THE WIELDER

Julie Falango

TABLE OF CONTENTS

Chapter 1 1

Chapter 2 14

Chapter 3 19

Chapter 4 30

Chapter 5 35

Chapter 6 52

Chapter 7 60

Chapter 8 68

Chapter 9 80

Chapter 10 86

Chapter 11 103

Chapter 12 123

Chapter 13 138

Chapter 14 156

Chapter 15 175

Chapter 16 181

Chapter 17 192

Chapter 18 197

Chapter 19 219

Chapter 20 229

Chapter 21 239

1

Cole

15 Years Ago

I twiddled my thumbs together while I waited. I sat in an armchair that was twice my size and nearly swallowed me up.

I didn't mind coming to visit the castle with Dad at night when he had meetings with the Queen and the King. I thought it was pretty cool, actually.

But I wasn't allowed to tell anyone that I was here. My dad said I had to stay out of sight and not disturb any of the royals while he was working. So I stayed in his study room in the castle while he worked and passed the time with reading and drawing.

Oh, who am I kidding?

I quickly found all of the hidden passages in the castle and a secret set of hallways in the walls that went everywhere. In my dad's study, there was a door hidden in the wall that I only discovered because I had tripped over the plush carpet a few months ago, falling directly into it. After that, I loved to come here and explore.

I have never encountered anyone in the passageways, so I assumed that they weren't really used anymore.

I hopped off the armchair and pushed on the secret wall that revealed the hallway behind it. The wall creaked as it opened and I froze, listening. I listened out in the hallway, but didn't hear anything. I wanted to make sure, so I tiptoed over to the door leading out of my dad's study and listened.

Several muted voices greeted me and I hurried to close the secret door, plop myself back in my armchair and look innocent.

But no one entered the study.

I frowned as the minutes ticked by and still, no one entered the study.

I decided that it was a false alarm. Without wasting any more time, I climbed out of my chair, wandered into the secret hallway, and turned left.

As I was heading down the narrow hallway, I heard those same voices again. I followed them into an alcove and approached a vent that was at my ankle level. I lowered onto my stomach and peered through the slits of the vent.

As I peered through the vent, I could see the feet of two people. One of the people was a man who had on long pants and fancy pointed shoes with laces tied in neat bows. The other was a woman, and she wore black, shiny shoes that elevated her heels off the ground and clicked when she walked. They looked impossible to walk in.

"Will your husband be joining us, Your Highness?" the male voice asked.

My eyes widened. I knew that voice, of course, because it belonged to my dad.

"No, Franklin," the female voice replied, who I decided had to be the Queen because my dad wouldn't address just anyone as Your Highness. "He will be putting the girls to bed now so let's discuss before he returns."

"Understood," my dad said. "Please, let's sit."

I shifted for a better view and watched as they crossed the room and took seats in armchairs opposite each other. They sat in front of an extravagant brick-lined fireplace that had a faint glow.

My dad sat with his back straight and his hands in his lap looking at the Queen. I finally got my first glimpse at the ruler of the kingdom we lived in.

She was really very pretty. Her hair was twisted on top of her head and her crown sparkled and reflected the slowly fading fire in the fireplace. She crossed her ankles and smoothed her red dress and looked at my dad like she was waiting.

My dad took a deep breath and leaned in.

"There are rumors, Camilla, of someone who will remove you from power," he said.

Her eyebrows furrowed and her color-stained lips turned into a thin line she leaned in.

"Excuse me?" she asked. "I have spent my entire reign strengthening the Royal Command in order to protect myself and the throne."

"I understand, Your Highness. The rumor is mostly credible though," my dad said.

"From who? Who is your source?" The Queen demanded.

There was a pause before my dad answered.

"A traveling visionary. She was passing through our kingdom and she came to the castle. The guards stopped her and they called me as she was speaking nonsense," my dad explained.

"A visionary?" the Queen asked. "How can we believe what she says is true?"

My dad sighed.

"This is not the first time we have interacted with this woman," he answered slowly. "She has appeared several times over the years and offered knowledge, wisdom, advice... which I have taken and passed to you. Every time it has worked out favorably."

The Queen let out a little laugh. "You are telling me that I made you my most trusted advisor, yet your advice came from an unknown woman?"

"I am not proud of my deceit. But some examples were when I warned you of the terrible storm system years ago and our actions saved thousands of our people. That, and other times we've deployed the ORC out of the kingdom. Although they didn't turn up anything, whatever threat was approaching us was fearful of our numbers and retreated."

The Queen put her manicured hand on her chin. "Franklin, all of these strategic moves I made under your guidance and they paid off," she said. "Despite the deceit, I do trust you. What did this woman tell you this time?"

My dad rose from his chair and opened the door leading out of the room. He left the door open and returned to his seat across from the Queen.

A few moments later, guards dressed in all black entered the room escorting a small, frail old woman. They kept a short distance behind her, never touching her.

She had pin straight hair that was a mixture of thin gray and white strands extending more than halfway down her back. She wore a long brown cloak and shuffled in the room with her head down.

"Are you the visionary?" the Queen asked the woman. She waved at the two guards and they left the room, closing the door behind them.

The woman lifted her head and looked at the Queen and my dad.

"*The light will be gone, you will all move on,*" the woman said.

"*The one you'll call your second,*

will be the force to be reckoned,

and although they are your own,

they will expel you from the throne."

The woman turned her head from the Queen and looked in my direction. I felt like she could see right through the wall and the vent and see me lying here on the ground eavesdropping. I held my breath.

"Franklin, what does that mean?" the Queen asked my dad.

He sighed. "It seems that the threat to your throne and your rule... will be from your second born," he replied, rubbing his eyes.

The Queen suddenly rose from her seat. "Alexandria?" she asked. She turned her gaze to the old woman and towered over her. "She is but a child."

"Gone before the twenty-first hour,

they pose no threat to your power."

That was the last thing the old woman stated before she turned away from them. She pulled open the door as her cloak spun behind her and left the room.

"Let her go," my dad said. He pulled out a paper and handed it to the Queen. "I wrote it all down so we could analyze it."

"There is no need. I heard her. Alexandria is going to be the one who dethrones me if I don't act," the Queen said.

"Ma'am, she is a child, as you said. She poses no threat," my dad said.

"Not if she's gone before... nine o'clock? That's the twenty-first hour," the Queen said looking at the grandfather clock on the wall behind her.

"Gone?" My father asked.

"No one, and I mean *no one* will remove me from power. I have dedicated my life to seeing to that."

"But your daughter?"

"I guess I was blessed with two daughters for this reason," the Queen said, void of emotion.

She turned to my dad.

"Franklin, intercept Nicholas and keep him occupied," she said. She stopped pacing and stared down at the fire, tossing the paper my dad had handed her into the small flame. It quickly ate up the paper and the fire popped and sent a few sparks up. "I have to go... take care of something."

"But Your Highness..." my dad started.

"Do you value your job, Franklin?" The Queen asked. "And the home you are able to provide for your family?"

My dad lowered his head. "Yes, my Queen."

"Then you have your assignment," she replied as my dad lowered his head. I got a glimpse of his sad face before I was unable to see his features anymore.

The two adults strode from the room and I stayed where I was on the floor in the secret hallway. I quickly scrambled to my feet and turned around.

I let out a yell at the sight of the old woman standing before me in this secret tunnel.

"Please don't hurt me," I said instinctively.

"*Go far beyond and above,*
for this girl you will grow to love.
If you exit her through the front gate,
you will save her from her fate," the old woman riddled at me. She turned away from me and backed out of the alcove.

My heart was pounding in my chest.

"Wait!" I called and shuffled out of the alcove after her.

But the woman was gone.

I closed my eyes and replayed her words in my head. It *sounded* like I was destined to interfere with the Queen's plan and save the princess.

But who was I? The son of one of the Royal Advisors? I had no power here. What was I going to do?

I decided I was certainly not going to let anything happen to an innocent girl because of something that old woman said.

I took off running down the narrow hallway, determined to find the princess and warn her.

As I ran, I realized two things. One, I didn't know who Alexandria was or what she looked like and two, I also didn't know where I was going.

It felt like I had been running through these halls for at least an hour. I went upstairs, downstairs, around long curved bends and still didn't find any princess.

I leaned on the wall and put my hands on my knees trying to catch my breath. It didn't help that I was wearing a buttoned up shirt and sweater with nice pants that my dad had made me wear in case anyone in the castle did see me. I pulled the sweater over my head and tied it around my waist, wiping the sweat off my forehead as I did so.

It was then that I heard the shouting.

I stood up and followed the shouting, tracing my hand along the wall as I moved.

"Help! Help! I'm stuck!" The voice shouted. I stopped in my tracks.

"Where are you!" I called back but got no answer.

I spun around and noticed a little bit of what looked like smoke seeping out from the wall. As I approached it, I realized there was a seam in the wall where there must be a hidden door, like the one in my dad's study.

With no obvious doorknob, I did the next best thing... I stepped back and delivered a kick to the wall. It bent inward but didn't open completely, and black smoke billowed out of the small opening I made. I could already feel the heat building and knew there was a fire behind this wall.

I took a couple more steps back and shouldered the door. I repeated the action several times and felt like the door was beginning to get ready to swing open.

After one last hard shove, the door gave way, toppling over whatever structure had been in front of the door and hitting the ground with a *crash!*

As I got to my feet, I took in the seriousness of the situation. The entire room was on fire and the heat was nearly unbearable. The smoke was thick and black and I immediately began coughing.

Crack!

I looked up to see one of the ceiling beams break off and come down towards me fast and fiery. I dove to the side and rolled away from where the beam landed near where I was before, taking one of the curtains down with me as I did so.

From my position on my stomach, I picked up my head and I saw her lying on the ground. Her brown hair was a mess and covered her face, so I could only hope she was still alive.

"Hello! Are you okay?" I called to her as I wrapped the curtain around myself to protect my skin and crawled over in her direction. She didn't respond to me.

By the time I got to her, I saw why.

Part of the flaming ceiling lay on her small body and I could see the fire touching her skin, changing its color instantly and filling my nose with a horrible burning smell.

I immediately reached for her and tried to pull her out but the weight was too great and I realized that I had to move the beam first.

I balled up my sweater and positioned it against my arm and shoulder and shoved it, pushing it off of her. When it hit the ground next to her, hot embers showered on me but I ignored the sizzle as they hit my exposed skin.

I took the fallen curtain and covered her with it, trying to douse the fire that was ablaze on her purple dress. I patted her body hoping to put the flames out quicker.

I removed the curtain and looked at her. Half of her dress was completely burned and so was her back. The skin was red, peeling, and angry. But I had to stop wasting my time and get her out of here.

I laid the curtain down on the ground and rolled her body onto it. Her eyes were closed when I rolled her over and her face was pretty. Her dark hair had been basically singed off and I only hoped it would grow back for her.

I tugged on the curtain and began to drag her body across the room towards the secret wall. I felt myself sweating and I felt the smoke sticking in my lungs as I began coughing again.

I scooped the girl up in my arms and escaped out the wall I had previously busted through. I pulled the door shut in an effort to keep some of the smoke from spilling into the hallway before lying her back on the curtain.

What had that old woman said? Go out the front gate? It seemed a little bold to just walk out the front door with this girl who had just had an attempt on her life... by the Queen no less!

"But which way is out?" I asked as I dragged the lifeless princess behind me. I tried to remember which way I had come but I realized I went through every hallway here and was hopelessly lost. But I continued on.

I was slowly trudging down a staircase when I heard commotion up ahead. I gently crept down the rest of the staircase with my guest in tow until I reached the bottom and approached a door there.

I pushed it open and peered into the... kitchen, it would seem like. I pulled Princess Alexandria through the kitchen until we reached the door at the other end. This door led outside and I was eager to feel fresh air, but I was also exhausted from dragging this girl through half of the castle. I just had to figure out how to get her out through the front gate.

The door swung open and smacked me in the face as I tumbled backwards. I sat up and put my body in front of Alexandria protectively. I realized that she was a stranger to me, but after saving her life, I felt obligated to protect her until she was safe.

"What are you doing here?" The woman who opened the door asked. She had glasses and long black hair that went to her shoulders. Her eyes examined me. "Aren't you Franklin Monahan's son?"

I nodded silently.

Her eyes went from me to the body behind me. She pushed past me and dropped to her knees next to the princess.

"What did you do?" She asked, examining the girl's body.

"I... I saved her," I said. "Please don't hurt her."

"I'm a doctor, sweetie, I will help her," she said. "How did you know where she was?"

"I didn't, I searched for her. There was an old lady..." I started.

"You saw the visionary?" The doctor asked me.

I nodded again. "But I didn't tell anyone," I added fearfully. Behind her glasses, her eyes were trusting but I was still afraid of the trouble I would get into.

"I will take Alexandria with me, and I will heal her. This will be our secret and all of our lives will depend on it. Do you understand, Mr. Monahan?" She asked. I nodded and she continued, "We also have to pretend we never met tonight. I know this is scary, but you will be safer and she will be safer if this is the case."

"Yes, ma'am," I said. I started to say something else but I held my tongue. The woman seemed to notice.

"What's wrong? Are you hurt?" she asked me.

"No, I'm... I'm fine," I answered. "Just try to... um, get her out through the front gate."

"Good thinking, Mr. Monahan. I will hide her in the back of my jeep, head out that way since I won't be searched and take her to my home," she explained. "You did a very brave and noble thing here, saving a life. Now, let me take you to your father. I'll cover up this mess."

I felt some tears fill my eyes. I saved a life today.

I hoped I would get to see the princess again, especially because that old lady said I would grow to love her one day. She was very pretty, and I intended to keep that promise.

"Thank you, Doctor," I said as she reached down and put her hands on my shoulders.

"I'm Dr. Palmer, and you're welcome," she said.

2

Cole
Now

I opened my eyes as I relived the memory of rescuing Lexi over and over in my head. I didn't regret it then and I don't regret it now. What I did regret was falling asleep with my arm underneath me on the hard concrete floor because it ached.

I didn't know how much time had passed since Queen Camilla had me tossed in the cellar jail after revealing the truth to Lexi. I now regretted all of the years that Remy and I kept it a secret from her.

But when exactly was a good time to tell someone that they were royalty, but it had to stay a secret because otherwise the Queen, their *mother,* would try to kill them... again?

I sighed and sat up, and leaned against the wall of my cell.

The cell was small, dark, and cold. A few lights lit the hallway and shed some light in my cell through the iron bars that kept me inside. There was a wooden bench against one wall and that was it.

I had woken up on the floor and that's where I stayed. I felt no need to move or get up. My life was effectively over now that I was labeled as a traitor and charged with treason.

It was definitely too optimistic to think that Lexi was okay. Without anyone there to defend her, I assumed that either Camilla or Nate just finished the job after I had been knocked out. Why would she keep her around after trying to kill her fifteen years ago?

A long creak followed by a jingling sound alerted me that someone was entering the dungeon and coming my way. When I had woken earlier, there was a cup of water and half of a sandwich waiting for me, so I was hopeful this guest would bring me another meal. My stomach was rumbling a little bit anyway.

If this was my life and what I had to look forward to, these next few years here were going to be long ones.

I listened as the footsteps descended down into the dungeon and got closer to me. I stood up and inched closer to the bars trying to see who was coming. I secretly hoped it would be Lexi, that she was still alive so that I could tell her the truth. Whether or not she believed me would be a different story.

As the visitor stepped in front of my cell, my shoulders tensed a little bit. It was not the girl that I loved, but someone that shared her similar features.

"How. Dare. You," Damion said through gritted teeth. His voice was full of hate.

"Damion, listen. You don't know the full story," I said.

"You are lucky these bars are here because I would kill you myself," he said. He smacked his hands on the bars for effect, but I didn't flinch.

"Our entire lives, you've known she wasn't dead. You knew that day I met her, you knew during training, you knew *every year* on the anniversary of her death but you said nothing. Nothing!"

I continued to say nothing.

"You stole my sister from us! Alexandria's death destroyed my family and you probably laughed at our misery knowing she was alive and well. What was your plan, Monahan? What was the purpose of training her? To use her against us? Marry her and make a play for the throne?"

I took a step closer to Damion and he shuffled backwards a little bit, but was still within my range. I knew he felt safe with the bars between us, but unfortunately for him, no bars could keep me from Lexi.

"I saved her life," I replied calmly. "She got to live a normal life and I taught her to defend herself in case her mother ever tried to kill her again."

Damion laughed out loud. "My mother? Ha! You are delusional!"

"She was afraid of what Lexi would grow up to become. Lexi posed a threat to her power and she eliminated the threat... or at least, she tried to," I said. I clenched my fists at my side in anger. I never said any of this information out loud and it made me so mad to even think about it. "When I found Lexi in that room, she was literally on fire, burning alive. I pulled her out and got her to safety and I made a promise to keep her safe."

"That's some tale you've spun for yourself."

"And you've seen the scars on her back for yourself."

"*You* set the fire and *you* are the reason for those scars!" Damion was yelling again. He reached through the bars and grabbed my shirt and pulled me hard against the bars. I could have avoided it but I figured I would give him this one.

"Is Lexi still alive?" I asked him.

"*Alexandria*," he sneered, emphasizing her real name, "is alive and well. She's out on an ORC mission as we speak."

"A mission?" I asked. "What type of mission?"

"You're no longer ORC, Cole," he said. "We don't have traitors in our command. You will spend forever down here and you will rot. You will wish that my mother would let me kill you, but unfortunately she wants you alive."

I suddenly reached up and grabbed Damion's shirt with my left hand and yanked him towards me. I used my right hand on the back of his head to pull it towards the bars and a vibrating *clang!* sounded as his frontal lobe smacked into the iron.

The impact echoed for a few seconds as Damion crumbled to the ground in front of my cell.

"Sorry, man," I said to his unconscious form as I bent down and started rifling through his pockets, my arms through the bars of my prison. I kept peeking to the side to see if anyone heard the noise and came running, but no one had appeared.

I finally heard the jingle in his ORC jacket pocket and pulled out the keyring he had.

I fiddled with the keys until I fit one into the lock outside my cell and the door swung open. I stepped out into the hallway and dragged Damion into the cell. I didn't want to, but I knew I was going to need quite the head start before Damion alerted someone of my escape.

He had said that Queen Camilla was keeping me alive and that Lexi was alive too. My only thought was that the Queen was using me as leverage against her, but for what reason, I didn't know.

I hoped to the heavens that my escape didn't alter anything and that she stayed safe. I felt my throat tighten a little at the thought of never seeing her again, but I vowed that I would. I was going to leave, recruit help and return to rescue her for a second time.

I looked at Damion's fallen form. The poor guy was hurting emotionally with this new information, and now physically too that I had just knocked him out. I shimmied his ORC jacket off of him and put it on. It fit pretty well since we had similar builds.

I locked him in the cell and took the keys with me as I ascended the stairs towards the door that would take me towards my freedom, but also farther away from the girl I loved.

3

Lexi

The wind whipped past my face and blew my braided hair behind me as we sped forward. I held onto Nate (unwillingly and only to keep myself from flying off) as he pushed us onward on an ORC-issued bike as we headed towards an unknown destination.

I was not privy to the location of my first ORC mission. All I knew was that we were going to look for and retrieve what they called a "person of interest".

A few days had passed since the revelation of my true identity and I witnessed an unconscious Cole Monahan dragged away before my eyes. I still hadn't fully accepted the truth, and I wouldn't respond immediately when people called me Alexandria, so I was still introducing myself as Lexi.

The Queen was not pleased that I was still using the name Lexi, but she hadn't done anything to punish me... yet.

After they dragged Cole away, she told me that as long as I did what she asked, he would not be killed. She said that she would grant me a visit to see him after a week if I proved useful on this mission, and also kept my mouth shut about our conversations.

I, of course, agreed in order to keep him alive.

Nate was given the title as my handler, which meant I reported to him, and he followed me around, making sure I didn't make a run for it. Not that I would with Cole locked up somewhere in the castle.

I searched every night through the tunnels and the passageways, but I never found any access to a basement or a cellar. I anticipated it being locked if I did find something, but I would've figured that problem out if I ever found the so-called cellar.

Queen Camilla and Nate reassured me that Cole was alive and I hoped they weren't lying to me. He was my weakness, so I did as I was told. If he was dead, I wouldn't do a single thing she asked of me.

She told me that she had big plans for me, which made me nothing but nervous. I didn't trust her as far as I could throw her but I kept my head down and completed my duties.

My friends could not have been more excited to learn about my true identity, even if I still wasn't completely sold on it. I wanted to ask the one person who could answer my questions, but whom I had not been able to see since returning to the castle to bring Ally back home.

Remy.

I'm sure she was worried sick. It had been almost a week and she had not seen me or Cole, although I am sure she heard the news of the return of the princess, since it probably spread like fire. She and I had just been reunited and now I had been pulled away from her again back towards... this life that I seemed drawn to.

Ally cried an exceptional amount when she found out and Damion only cried a little bit. After he moved past processing the information, he exploded into a fit of anger and threatened to kill Cole multiple times. Thankfully, the Queen forbade him from killing Cole but I made a mental note to try to follow Damion and see if he went to go see Cole. That is, if I could ever lose my own tail, Nate.

The most interesting meeting I had was with King Nicholas, my... father. He was the spitting image of Damion but with older and sadder eyes. I had read in that book about the royals that he blamed himself for her death... or rather, my death, so I am sure he has carried that burden on his shoulders for the past fifteen years.

When we first met, he hugged me awkwardly, but didn't have much to say. Our entire encounter probably lasted no more than five minutes. I was trying to give him, or anyone who needed it, the space to process all of this new information.

I returned my focus to our surroundings and felt myself bump around on the bike as we transitioned from smooth pavement to a dirt road. I looked up to see an old tree stump zoom past us on my one side. I whipped my head in the other direction and saw the unmistakable red dots of berries on the plants as we continued on ahead.

I knew exactly where we were as we drove through the familiar trees and the place I called home for the past fifteen years appeared right before my eyes.

The six bikes formed a semi-circle around the front door of mine and Remy's home and I held my breath. I moved to get off the bike and Nate put his hand on my leg and shook his head. He released his hand before I unkindly removed it for him and I stayed where I was.

Brayden was to our left and he dismounted his bike, wielding a larger version of those paint guns they had used on us during training. He took a few steps closer to the house.

"ORC!" he called with his weapon trained at the front door. "Come out now!"

The house was silent. I closed my eyes and listened.

I could hear Nate's heart pounding in his chest, the wind lightly rustling the leaves and the breathing of every ORC member around us, but nothing from within the house.

"ORC!" he repeated. "Last chance!"

He waited about five seconds before I saw his shoulder tense and he pulled the trigger. His weapon fired twice and it sent two small cylinders into my home, shattering the glass window as it went.

A small explosion of light went off inside and then the house started to fill with a white smoke. I was not going to let them burn my house down.

I shot myself off of the bike and ran towards the house. I made it as far as the steps leading up my porch before someone grabbed my jacket and yanked me back, throwing me onto the ground. I whacked my head on the ground and I felt tears coming to my eyes.

Brayden's face appeared above me.

"Woah, Lexi," Brayden said as he extended a hand. "I know you're new and eager to get inside but I just shot a flash bang and tear gas in there."

"Tear gas?" I asked, rubbing my irritated eyes.

He laughed and pulled me to my feet. "Yeah, I can see the small amount you were exposed to even got you. Sorry about that," he said, gesturing to the imprint of my body on the ground. "Now, stay here with Nate while we go search the place until we call all clear."

This version of Brayden that didn't absolutely hate me was a version of him I could get on board with. He had apologized profusely for his behavior during training and for shooting me at point-blank range. I wasn't mad at him and now I had someone on my side who was actually nice to me, unlike my rather nasty bodyguard.

Within seconds, Nate was at my side, glaring at me. "Don't run off," he said angrily. Whatever had happened that turned him into the Queen's personal pet and made him hate me more than I thought possible, was still a mystery.

"Gotta be quicker, I guess," I said with some sass and turned back to face my home.

I knew Remy wouldn't be inside. I didn't hear a sound so she was likely not there. Surely she heard the news of Princess Alexandria miraculously turning up alive and knew something was going on. Still, I continued to pray that she wasn't hurt inside until I heard an "all clear" yelled from Brayden to those of us waiting outside.

"Come on," Nate said, leading the way. "Let's go search the premises."

"What are we looking for?" I asked, trying to sound interested but not overly eager.

He didn't offer a response as he entered the house.

Rude.

I followed behind him and upon entering, the ORC members were tearing the place apart. I saw them opening every drawer and cabinet, slicing open the pillows on our couch, and turning over the cushions and the carpets. I wanted to scream at them, but I kept my cool. I wasn't sure anyone knew whose home this was as they ransacked it.

Nate left me alone but I knew he kept one eye on me, watching my movements. I sauntered down the hallway to my bedroom and peered inside. It had already been tossed by the ORC and everything that had been in my closet was all over the floor.

There was a painting on the wall that was crooked, probably half returned to its spot by an ORC member. But then I remembered that I did not have anything on the walls in my room. This painting wasn't mine.

It was a small painting of a rather lovely mountain range with the sun just peeking over the mountains. The colors that were splashed on the artwork made it look like it was sunrise. I removed the painting from the wall and flipped it over but there was nothing there.

I threw a quick look over my shoulder and popped the back of the flimsy frame off. On the back of the painting was Remy's beautiful cursive writing:

Don't trust Camilla. Find me here and I'll tell you the truth. I'm sorry you found out this way.

I turned over her note and stared at the mountains in the painting. I didn't know where they were or what they were called, so finding them wouldn't be easy but I understood her need for secrecy.

I folded the artwork and slid it up into my pant leg where I kept my knife so no one would find it on me. I poked my head out the door and the coast was clear, so I continued down the hallway.

Two ORC members were pulling on the basement door but Remy had locked it. She had locked it when I was younger so I didn't open it and tumble down there as a child. The two ORC members walked away mumbling something about needing special cutters to get the lock off.

As soon as they were out of sight, I stood on my toes and swiped the key from above the door frame. I clicked the lock open and descended into the basement. I flipped the switch to turn on the bare lighting down here that gifted me my excellent vision.

Nothing seemed out of place as I looked around, and the memories came flooding back. I learned my first sutures here, threw knives, fixed wounds and more in this dark basement.

I started going through the boxes of medical supplies we kept down here but everything appeared to be in place.

I pulled out a box labeled "burn supplies" and set it on the ground. I bet she had to restock this after treating me as a child with my burns.

My eye caught something left on the shelf tucked in the back. It was a small box with tattered edges, no larger than a shoebox. In fact, it was a shoebox and on the top of it was a piece of medical tape with one word written on it.

Alexandria.

I opened the box immediately. There wasn't much in it. A few scraps of ribbon and some purple fabric balled up. I pulled out the fabric and analyzed it. When I held it up, it resembled... a child's dress. It had hardly any back left to it. The edges were rough, black and... burnt.

I felt myself start to tear up and tried to blame it on the lingering tear gas, but I knew that wasn't the cause.

I knew deep in my heart that the stories were true.

I truly was Princess Alexandria, even though I didn't want to be.

They had taken me from the castle, I had been seriously injured and brought here to grow up with Remy and Cole by my side. The tears fell freely and I kneeled on the ground as I held the pieces of the dress between my fingers.

Suddenly, I was hit with a wave of what I assumed was a memory of someone tying my hair up in a neat bun with that ribbon that was in the box. I heard my father's voice calling my name as I crept through the castle searching for him.

"Alexandria. Alexandria!"

Someone put a hand on my shoulder and I whirled around.

"Alexandria? Are you all right?" an ORC member asked me. He was crouching behind me and his eyes were worried. Another ORC member stood behind him at the base of the steps. "Get the Lead," he called to the other, who took off up the stairs two at a time.

I turned my back to him and held my dress from fifteen years ago and cried. Loudly and audibly.

I felt that man rubbing my back gently while I sobbed as the reality of having my childhood ripped away from me finally sank in.

"What can I do to help you, Alexandria?" the man asked.

I turned to him as tears streamed down my red face.

"First, please call me Lexi," I said. "Second, tell me your name."

"I'm Luke, a medic," he answered. "I know you are a medic on this mission too, so I'm just here to support you."

"Thank you, Luke," I said to him as I curled up the dress and began putting it back in the box.

Brayden appeared in front of me.

"Lexi, what's wrong?" he asked. "Are you hurt? Luke, is she hurt?"

"Uh... emotionally would be my diagnosis," Luke answered.

"Smart ass," I said with a small smile.

"And cured by my humor," he added.

"I'm sorry, I'm fine," I said. "It was... just a lot to take in, that's all."

Brayden looked at the box in my hands.

"The dress, or what's left of it, that I was wearing the night of the fire," I answered and closed the top of the box. I held it close to me and stood up. "I didn't really want to believe any of it, but I guess I have to now."

"Did you find anything else?" Brayden asked.

"No, there's nothing but medical supplies down here," I replied.

"You searched every box?" someone called from the stairs.

Nate.

Great.

"No, but there's just supplies in them. Trust me," I answered and made my way to the stairs but Nate blocked me.

"You need to search them all," he said.

I squared up against him and narrowed my eyes.

"You and I both know why I was brought on this mission. You and I also know whose house this is, so it's safe to say you can trust me that it's all medical supplies," I said menacingly.

"Wait, who's house is this?" Luke asked from behind me.

"It's mine," I growled at Nate. "And the person of interest you're looking for, the woman who raised me? She's long gone."

Nate tried to speak up but I shouldered past him.

"I'm one of the best. And if she trained me, then obviously she *is* the best. You won't find her here," I added.

I trudged up the stairs, box in hand, and went to wait by the bikes. I had had enough emotional turmoil for today. I also decided that I would demand to see Cole today when we returned to get the answers that I needed, otherwise I would go crazy not knowing everything.

I stomped out of the place I called home for the past fifteen years and went to sit on Brayden's bike. I was annoyed at Nate, although that was not uncommon these days, and did not want to ride with him on the way back.

As the ORC members began to file out, I took one last look at my home. I was aware of the folded-up painting rubbing against the side of my leg and decided that I would make it my mission to find Remy in order to find out the truth.

Nate didn't argue when I sat behind Brayden and let him drive me back. I held onto him with one hand and onto the shoebox with another hand and we rode in silence as I stewed in my thoughts.

When we returned to the castle, there was a huge commotion. ORC members were running around every which way, with no method to their madness. Something was happening.

"Hey!" Brayden called to one of the guys running past as he hopped off the bike. He held it steady for me to climb off while still clutching my box. "What's going on?"

"You didn't hear? Cole Monahan escaped."

4

I stood in one of the many royal studies in the castle in front of the Queen. Ally stood on one side of me, while Damion stood on the other with a bag of ice on his face. Nate, my guard dog, as I had begun to affectionately refer to him as, stood by the door.

"We will find him, Mum," Damion said, muffled through the ice. "I'll lead the mission, myself."

"You know him well, Alexandria," the Queen said to me. "Where do you think he would go?"

"I don't know," I answered honestly.

I truly didn't know. I wanted answers just as much as anyone else in this room. I don't know why he would escape when I was here. Maybe everything had been a lie since the moment he and I met.

"Let me help track him," Ally piped up.

Like me, Ally had been granted an invitation to join the ORC due to our unique circumstances. She had excitedly joined the Scouts.

"No, honey. I need you here," the Queen said.

"Mum, I could be useful!" Ally countered. "I want to find him, too. He took my sister from me!"

"I'm sorry, Allyson. But what I say goes. You are dismissed," the Queen said.

Ally huffed and turned towards the door. Nate so graciously opened the door for her and sealed it again after her exit.

"I will take a small team. With Lexi's diverse skill set, I won't need as many people, plus I want to be able to move without being detected. We aren't sure what's waiting outside the kingdom," Damion began.

He removed the ice pack from his face so he could speak a little easier.

"I will take Lexi, Nate and Brayden from the Wielders, Daniel from the Scouts, and it will be Scott Yager and myself from the Combatants," he said.

I had yet to see my friend, Yager, since the night of the fire and I was looking forward to getting to see him again. I was happy to hear that he had made it into the ORC, although at his massive size, I had had few doubts.

"Fine. Leave in the morning," the Queen said. "Damion, you are dismissed."

Damion nodded his head and made his exit.

"Now Alexandria, Nate has reassured me that you played no part in Cole Monahan's escape, as you had been with him all day today and he has kept a watchful eye on you," the Queen said.

I rolled my eyes and then remembered whose presence I was in. What was she going to do? Threaten to kill Cole again when they find him? She held no power over---

Whack!

My hand flew to my face where she had just struck me and I took a step back. I opened my mouth to speak and no words came out.

"You will be respectful as you take my orders. Be the part and look the part. I made you and I own you now, not him or Dr. Palmer." The queen said Remy's professional name like it left a bad taste in her mouth. "Changing your last name to Palmeyer was cute, by the way."

"You knew?" I asked, crossing my arms.

"I am your mother, after all; I know my children. You have your father's traits, the dark brown eyes like Damion and you used to have darker hair like him too," she replied. "I investigated everyone in the castle that night, but Dr. Palmer wasn't scheduled to be here so I didn't question her at the time. She was just picking up some supplies." She paused. "I assume you found the proof you were looking for today?"

"Did you plant it? Is it even real? Is that why you sent me on that mission?" I asked angrily and clenched my fists at my sides. I realized I may have been a fool for thinking what I found was real.

"Oh, no. I wanted you to see the capture of Dr. Palmer but it seems that she, too, has slipped from our grasp. No matter. We will hunt Mr. Monahan and you will help. I will be keeping Allyson here as leverage for your return. If you don't come back and you try to run off into the sunset with him, she dies."

She said it so simply, like taking a life was that easy.

"You wouldn't hurt your own daughter," I said quietly.

"Tell that to the handprint on your face, child," the Queen answered with a nasty grin. "My daughter died a long time ago. Damion is my first child and Allyson is my second. You are merely a tool to do my bidding." That stung more than the slap. She continued, "Nate will give me regular reports on your activity and ensure you stay in line. He has been authorized to use... whatever means necessary."

I felt a shiver run up my spine. Remy's note was right to not trust the Queen. She was a wild card and unpredictable.

I don't know what I did - besides getting kidnapped as a child - that provoked such hatred toward me. I had asked her multiple times that night that they took Cole away but she had dodged the question. Perhaps she only wanted one daughter, and now she was used to living life without me. She basically said as much.

It was a miracle that I even woke up every day living in this castle with her. One call and I could be thrown in the cellar in Cole's place. But she said I was to do what she asked and those I cared about would not be harmed. It would be a welcome excuse to get out of here, even if my departure was for a mission to hunt the man I love.

Or the man I used to love.

I didn't know what I felt anymore. Our friendship was true, but something broke inside me this morning when I saw the ashes of the dress that I had been wearing the night of the fire. My heart shattered in that moment and the pain was fierce. Everytime that I thought about what I had lost and missed out on, my heart hurt.

I wasn't sure if anything could be done to mend the broken pieces.

Now or ever.

"You are dismissed," the evil Queen finally said to me, and I wasted no time hurrying away from her.

5

The Queen did not come to see us off in the morning... thankfully.

Damion and I had spent the previous evening filling bags of food and water for our mission. It didn't have an end date which was a little scary so we packed as much as we could fit into the jeep we would be taking.

We had talked and laughed about our first meeting now that we had learned of our familial relationship. We joked about what our lives may have been like had I grown up with them in the castle and not with Cole. That brought back the familiar ache in my heart.

Damion asked me a lot about Cole and Remy, although he, like everyone else, referred to her as Dr. Palmer. My answers and stories were honest.

I had a positive experience growing up. I was glad they taught me the things that they had and I enjoyed my life living with them. I wasn't really sure where my life would take me now that I didn't have them as my family anymore, and it seemed like the Queen didn't want me as her family either. Maybe after we tracked down Cole and got the truth out of him, I could move on with my life.

The sun was beginning to paint the sky warm hues of pink and yellow as it threatened to reveal itself, which meant it was almost time.

We loaded up the jeep and would be taking four bikes with us. Damion and I would be riding in the jeep, much to Nate's dismay. He tried to put up a fight, claiming he was in charge of keeping me safe, per the Queen but Damion squashed that right away. I owed him one for that.

Damion and Brayden were both going to be the Team Leads for this mission, which was probably a good idea since my brother was going to be *slightly* biased toward destroying Cole if we found him. We thought Brayden might show... more restraint.

I was sitting in the passenger seat with my feet hanging out the side waiting for our team to arrive. We were waiting on Yager and Daniel to get their ORC bikes from storage. I wished I would've got to ride one of the bikes and feel that freedom instead of co-piloting the jeep.

We learned that when Cole escaped, he had taken my bike and rode off with it, Remy's bow and arrow, and another one of my knives that were in the storage compartment. I didn't appreciate him taking those away from me. I didn't appreciate a lot of the things he took from me actually.

I heard the rumble of engines as two figures in all black rolled up to us on their bikes. I could see the blue stripe on one of them, which was obviously Yager since he was huge, and the green stripe for the Scouts on the smaller figure's arm, which had to be Daniel.

Yager stopped his bike, pulled off his helmet and shook out his head and hair dramatically.

"Princess Big Shot!" he yelled to me, probably waking up the whole kingdom at this early hour.

I smiled at him and waved.

"Good to have you back! I'm stoked to be going out on this mission with you. We're going to find that scumbag and roast him alive!" Yager shouted.

"Alright, settle down. We would prefer he's alive for questioning," I said honestly. But also, I'm not sure I could watch someone take a life, especially not Cole's life.

"That's everyone," Damion called. "He took Lexi's bike when he left so we're going to follow the trail that leads out of the gardens and away from here. If and when the trail ends, Daniel, you can lead and try to see if you can track him, got it?"

Daniel nodded with his helmet on so the movement was big and slow and it seemed to slide around his head.

"Earpieces in," Damion commanded as he handed me one.

They were small and the coolest things I had ever seen. We wore them in our ears and we could talk to each other if we needed to when they were on. Each of us carried a set of handheld radios, that he called walkie-talkies, which I couldn't help but think would have been so fun for Cole and me to have as kids. I wished he would've snagged some from the ORC for us to play with when we were younger.

I shook the thoughts of him out of my head as Luke, the medic from our mission yesterday came up to me.

"You ready?" he asked with his big, blue eyes. "I packed you an extra medical bag in case you need it, but I've heard you do great work with just about anything."

I smiled at Luke. He was kind and thoughtful and genuinely seemed to care about me and the people on our team.

"Good luck out there," Luke said as he backed away. He was just delivering the extra medical supplies; but wouldn't be joining us on this mission, since we didn't need two medically trained individuals. It would have been nice to have another friendly face to balance out Nate.

"Thanks. We'll see you soon," I replied.

I turned and looked at the castle before getting in the jeep. Through an open window on the second floor, I caught a glimpse of King Nicholas watching us load up. He lifted his hand in a wave but showed no emotion on his face. I gave him a wave back and he withdrew from the window.

Poor guy. Guilt can consume you from the inside out. I was going to try to make amends and build our relationship when we returned. It was the least I could do.

I got in the jeep and pulled the door shut.

"You ever drive one of these?" I asked Damion.

"Of course," he answered and shifted us into gear and we were off.

Nate and Brayden stayed close behind us, followed by Yager and Daniel bringing up the rear. He wasn't going very fast and seemed to wobble a little bit until he got off of the rocky drive and onto the solid road.

I sighed and stared out the window as we rolled along.

"What's wrong?" Damion asked me. "I'm surprised your adrenaline isn't sending you through the roof."

I decided to be honest with him.

"The confusion and the heartache are canceling out the adrenaline," I answered. I held up a hand to silence my brother as he tried to cut me off. "I know you hate him and believe me, I feel... some type of way about him too. But I have loved him for fifteen years. It doesn't just go away overnight."

Damion was quiet for a while before he responded.

"Your death was the worst thing I had ever gone through," he said quietly. "I threw myself into training and into the ORC. I was so obsessed with being the best, recruiting the best, and having the best team so that nothing like that ever happened again. When I thought Ally had died in that cabin fire, I almost couldn't go on."

"Well, you did recruit the best," I said, looking at him with a big smile. "And she and I made it out of that fire just fine."

"Do you think Cole set that fire too?" Damion asked, his knuckles turning white on the steering wheel.

"No, I don't. Actually, I have no idea who could have done it. Perhaps a jealous recruit, but no one has made a second attempt since I've been back," I answered.

"Dammit, I didn't even think about that. Can't trust anyone now."

"I trust you, and I trust our team," I said and then remembered that Nate was on the team and I did not trust him.

"Bet you don't trust that hound that Mum assigned to keep an eye on you," Damion said quietly. Then he burst into laughter. I had to laugh too, surprised that he could sense that I didn't trust Nate. "She said it's to keep you safe now that you are in the royal family."

I laughed again at that comment. She and I both knew why Nate was babysitting me at all hours of the day. So that I stayed in line and didn't tell anyone about me selling my soul to her in exchange for the safety of Cole's and now Ally's lives - the most twisted version of bribery I've ever witnessed.

"Feel free to close your eyes and rest. I don't know what we'll encounter outside of the kingdom," my brother added.

I decided I might just take him up on that offer. I had hardly slept last night with my nerves running wild in anticipation of today. I patted the pocket that was on the side of my leg where I had the painting that Remy had written on to ensure it was still there. I had stared at it so long yesterday, I had committed it to my brain and I could see it when I closed my eyes.

Hopefully soon, I'd see Remy again too.

I woke up a few hours later with a stiff neck from leaning on the window. I rolled my head around in an unsuccessful attempt to loosen it up. The scenery around us was largely the same. We were still on a single road surrounded by open land and some sporadic trees. The sun had come up by now and was streaming in the window heating me up in my black attire.

"We just left the limits of the kingdom," Damion said to me since he saw that I was awake. "Our titles mean nothing to anyone who isn't from Odessa, so best not bring it up if we run into any folks."

"Do you anticipate running into anyone?" I asked.

Damion shrugged his shoulders.

"We're just not sure what's out here. The ORC is actually pretty defensive rather than offensive," he answered.

"That's surprising, considering who's running it," I mumbled.

"Huh?"

"Oh, nothing," I said quickly.

"Hold on, Daniel is slowing down," Damion said as he reduced our speed.

While I napped, Daniel must have taken the lead, as he was now in front of our jeep, while the other three brought up the rear in a neat "V" formation.

The road up ahead was splitting and heading in two different directions and we were going to have to pick one way to head in.

Daniel stopped at the split and looked both ways. I saw him dismount from his bike but leave it running and inspect the road, presumably looking to see if there were any tire marks that Cole's bike... I mean, *my* bike would've left behind.

After a few minutes, he seemed satisfied and got back onto his bike and turned to the left. Our caravan followed him wordlessly and off we went.

The time passed slowly as we continued onward. This road was winding around patches of forest, up and down through hills, and getting less and less smooth by the minute.

We were transitioning from a flat, paved road to a dirt road and my body was not pleased as I bumped around inside of the jeep. Our colleagues on bikes had taken up location in front of us as our tires tended to kick up a lot of dirt behind us.

"Can you radio to Daniel to tell him to try to find someplace for us to rest for the night? I don't want us to be big targets, driving with our lights on," Damion asked me.

I pressed my finger against the radio in my hand and held it to my mouth. "Daniel, find us a place to stop for the night," I said. "Over."

Damion laughed at me.

"What!"

"Nothing," he answered. "It was funny when you said 'over.'"

I saw Daniel give us a gloved thumbs up and speed ahead. His head swiveled from side to side as he examined the wooded areas looking for a place for us to set up camp.

He pointed his arm up and to the right with his pointer finger to signal us towards a pushed-back area of woods.

He slowed down and maneuvered his bike off the road and towards the trees. The bikes were able to get through the treeline but Damion and I in our jeep were not able to. He spun the jeep around and backed us up towards the trees to tuck as much of the vehicle in the foliage as he could before putting us in park and turning off the jeep.

I jumped out of the car and my legs wobbled a little bit after their full day of inactivity. Damion was by my side quickly like an overprotective big brother.

"Let's set up some sleeping arrangements first, before we lose the rest of this sunlight then settle in and have something to eat," he said.

The boys all dismounted their bikes and pulled what looked like camping supplies out of the storage units in the bikes.

Yager propped his helmet on his bike and his hair was pressed to his forehead with sweat. He flashed me a smile with perfectly white teeth and began pulling out roll-up mats for us to sleep on.

Brayden pulled out fabric that must be some version of a tent and so did Nate. They each pitched a tent next to each other for us to sleep in. It wasn't clear what the sleeping arrangements were going to be, considering there were six of us and I was the only girl, but I was willing to be flexible as long as I didn't have to sleep anywhere near Nate.

Daniel seemed to be having trouble setting up his tent. He was fiddling with the poles and trying to make it stand upright but it kept falling over.

"Dude, take your helmet off. You can't see in that thing," Yager called to him but he didn't listen. He was determined to set up this tent by himself.

Yager finished setting up his own tent and approached Daniel to help him.

"Come on man, let me help you," Yager said and tried to take the fabric from him but Daniel wouldn't budge. "I'm telling you, you'd see better with your helmet off."

Yager grabbed Daniel's helmet and yanked upward pulling it off of his head.

A long golden braid fell out and I gasped as I took in the sight of the person we all thought had been Daniel guiding us.

It was not Daniel.

"Oh my gosh," I said quietly.

It was Ally.

"What's wrong?" Damion asked, turning around. "Oh my gosh."

"Ally?" I said and closed the distance between us. "What are you doing here?"

She brushed her braid over her shoulder now that it was free from being stuck in her helmet.

"I'm here for the mission!" she answered. "I couldn't let you guys go and have all of the fun while I sat at home. I've been doing that for fifteen years!"

"Allyson!" Damion yelled. "Mum is going to kill me!"

I realized that the Queen's bargaining chip to keep me in line was here with us. Everyone I cared about was either on the run or here in our group. I stole a glance at Nate; he looked angry, and also unsure of what to do. I dared him to try and threaten Ally in the presence of her brother.

"Well, I am so stoked that you are here!" Yager said excitedly and scooped her up into a hug. "Now let me set up your tent, little lady."

Ally stepped over to me and hugged me unexpectedly, while Yager constructed her tent.

"I thought you could use a friend in all this," she whispered so only I could hear.

"Thank you," I whispered back to her. I held onto her for an extra second. I was thankful for her presence. She knew how close Cole and I were as she had seen it firsthand before they took him away from me. She was right; I could use a friend.

"All set," Yager called and gestured behind himself to the now assembled sleeping quarters. "Now, where's the grub? I'm starving!"

Damion retrieved our food pack from the back of our vehicle and passed out several of the food bars and pieces of fruit we had packed ourselves.

While we sat in a group amongst the tree roots and fallen leaves, Ally recounted her tale of how she joined us on this mission. The shy and scared girl I had met on the first day of ORC training was gone and now a strong and brave individual stood in her place.

She told us how she went to see Daniel before we headed out and gave him a solid knock to the back of the head with his own helmet. We all chuckled when she said he was going to wake up in an equipment storage closet in the garage where all of the ORC bikes were kept.

I glanced over at Nate. He seemed to be lost in thought, but would occasionally throw in a laugh or a smile to please everyone. I wondered what he was thinking now that Ally, his bargaining chip was here. I'm sure he was looking for an opportunity to radio into the Queen to tell her that her daughter was here... or at least the daughter that she still cared about was.

We had lit a few lanterns in the middle of our circle after deciding that lighting a fire would draw too much attention. They were the sole sources of light now that the sun had set and we were all beginning to feel the exhaustion of the day.

"Alright, let's get some rest everyone," Damion announced after a while. "Who will take the first watch?"

"I will," Nate answered quickly.

"Good. Thanks, Nate," Damion said. "I guess with Allyson here now, she and Lexi can share a tent, and then we will all pair up in the others."

We all settled into our respective tents to get some sleep before we had to get up early tomorrow to continue our mission to find Cole and my secret mission to find Remy, wherever she may be.

I waited for Ally to fall asleep before quietly unzipping my tent and sneaking out into the woods. I threw on my bag, my birthday gift from Cole, and silently slid my knife into my ankle holster. I was wearing my ORC tactical gear to try to stay hidden and for this reason, I went without any additional weapons, like my bow.

I crept along through the trees slowly, dodging any low-hanging branches or leaves to avoid making any rustling sounds and alerting Nate to my approach.

I stopped moving, closed my eyes, and listened.

I heard the slight rustle of nature as the breeze pushed it around, the scurrying of whatever small creatures were awake at night and were probably watching me right now, and then I heard the gentle crunch of footsteps and knew I was getting close.

I opened my eyes and continued onward, following my senses that guided me.

The woods were dark but I could thank Remy for my trained eyes that helped me navigate through the trees. They loomed around me tall and ominous but I dug some courage out, knowing I needed to see what Nate was up to if I wanted to guarantee the safety of Ally and our group.

I had considered telling her and Damion about her being used as leverage to get me to cooperate and do the Queen's bidding, but I doubted that either one of them would believe me. The Queen had said if I told anyone, she would kill Cole and then Ally, but now with Cole missing and Ally here with me, I might be able to protect her.

It wasn't like I could stay up all night to watch her, in case Nate tried something, but I knew I was going to have to think of something.

I stopped my forward progress when I heard the crackle of a radio and Nate's hushed voice.

"Regrettably, yes," Nate was saying. "Obviously, I wasn't expecting her arrival."

I stayed low to the ground and clung close to a tree to shield me as I peeked my head around it to get a glimpse of him.

He was pacing between two trees up ahead and was holding the radio in front of his face.

"Do you anticipate her being a problem?" the radio crackled and although it was a quiet voice, I had no doubts that it was Queen Camilla on the other end.

"Alexandria is smart, she proved that during our training," Nate said into the radio. "But with Allyson here, I fear I have lost my control over her."

I let out a quiet scoff at that comment and then threw my hand over my mouth. Nate was still pacing although he threw his eyes in my general direction for a second before they returned to the ground he was walking on.

"She might run off to find Monahan, and you could follow her once she does," Queen Camilla said. "He is the one we need. He knows the truth."

"What are your orders?" Nate asked.

"She could've been an asset if this had played out differently... but I always knew she would have to go in the end," Queen Camilla answered. "Eliminate her quietly."

"Which one, Your Majesty?" Nate asked.

"Alexandria."

My eyes widened in fear and surprise at the order to remove me from the equation.

"And keep it efficient. I was young and sloppy with starting that fire fifteen years ago, so perhaps something cleaner," the Queen's voice added through the radio.

"Yes, ma'am," Nate said quietly and lowered the radio from his face.

I kneeled on the ground and placed my left hand on the trunk of the tree to stabilize myself as the tears fell freely and silently. I was struggling to process, yet again, new and shocking information. She admitted to Nate that she set that fire that almost killed me as a child, but I could not fathom any reason why. Why me and not Ally or Damion? Why not all of us if she didn't want children anymore? Were they even safe around her?

I was reminded of the greeting she gave Ally after I had brought her home after the cabin fire. She had shown sincerity and concern for the well-being of her daughter. Now I think I understood why Queen Camilla acted the way she did towards me. She thought she succeeded and that I had been dead for the past fifteen years while I lived safely with Remy.

My heart sank.

Remy and Cole and all of their comments about keeping me safe over the years and avoiding the ORC all made sense now. They were keeping me away from her, protecting me, and training me to protect myself in case they were unable to, like right now.

I was fairly certain that I believed that comment that the Queen made about setting the fire. I felt sadness and betrayal that even though I don't remember any of it now. I had only been five years old when that woman tried to kill me. I had been completely defenseless as a child.

I thought of the scars on my body which I now knew were caused by my own mother.

The sadness I was feeling turned to anger with that realization. I realized that she had taken my childhood from me, my chance at growing up with siblings, my chance at being normal and not covered in scars.

And I was angry.

I needed to find Cole and Remy more than ever and tell them that I knew the truth and we could go somewhere far away together.

I wiped away some of my tears and I realized that if I ran with Cole and Remy, I would be leaving behind my newly found siblings. Choosing between my two families would be an impossible choice. I decided that first I had to get away from Nate, now that he had new orders that didn't involve just keeping me in line. If I wasn't alive, I wouldn't even get the opportunity to make the choice of choosing between my two families.

I lifted my head up and peered back to where Nate was. He was now gone and presumably headed back to our camp to find me, trying to get the job done before anyone else woke up.

I did a quick survey of the area where he had been as I moved from my knees to my feet in a low crouch. I stood up slowly and turned to head back towards our camp.

Immense pain exploded in my right temple and my head whipped to the left as that side of me collided with the tree I had been next to.

I fell to the ground and shook my head and tried to get my bearings from whatever had just struck me.

"It's rude to eavesdrop," a voice above me said.

I opened my eyes to find Nate standing over me and smiling terribly.

I felt my brain still rattling inside my head but moved for my knife in my ankle holster.

Nate was quicker and stomped his foot onto my hand crushing it against the ground. I looked up at him and the last thing I saw was his fist flying towards my head before blackness took over.

6

I woke up in a world of pain and felt like my head had been split open.

At least I was waking up, so I wasn't dead... yet.

My body felt heavy and my arms and shoulders were sore, as well as my head where it had unkindly been tossed from side to side into equally hard objects courtesy of Nate Hogan.

I opened my eyes and I stood leaning against a tree, still surrounded by other trees so I knew Nate could not have moved me far. But then again, he knocked me out pretty good and I couldn't tell how much time had passed.

I realized that my wrists were bound together and suspended above my head. I followed the rope holding my hands together as it was tied to a thick branch above me.

Still looking up, I moved my feet and felt the pull on my shoulders as the ground sloped downward where I tried to maneuver. I backed myself back up against the tree and stood on its roots where I had started out.

I now looked down and realized that Nate must have positioned me here just a few inches higher than the ground level effectively trapping me in this spot unless I wanted to dislocate a shoulder.

"Dammit," I whispered to myself. I looked down and saw my empty ankle holster, knowing that he must have taken my knife from me while I was unconscious.

"Looking for this?" Nate's voice sounded from across the small clearing I was detained in. He covered the small space quickly and held my knife in one hand and my backpack in his other hand. He was breathing heavily and sweating.

I made to move towards him and remembered I was stuck in my spot by the tree. My impulsive move made him smile as he zipped my knife into my bag.

"You have so many skills that I had to outsmart you on short notice. This was the best I could do," he answered waving towards me and the rope holding me in place. "It actually worked out pretty well."

"Just get on with it, Nate. I don't have all day," I said, feigning bravery.

"Oh, I'm done now. I ran with your bag and your jacket a few miles up the road, dropping clues and supplies as I went that will give us a trail to follow," he explained.

I looked up again at my arms and realized they were indeed bare. I was just in my t-shirt and my jacket was missing.

"I'm going to tell them that you left in the night to find your precious Cole Monahan and I tried to follow you, but lost your trail. We will go on a wild chase to try to find you, but your body will be right here in the opposite direction no one thought to look."

I decided the best option was to stall and hopefully buy myself some time as I couldn't see another way out of this situation.

"What did I ever do to you, Nate?" I asked.

"I made you the Wielder that you are!" he answered angrily. "Sure, you had some good aim, but I taught you everything you needed to be an expert."

"Are you upset that I picked the Combatants over the Wielders?" I asked.

Nate frowned at me. "No," he answered. "I--."

"Jealous that I have skills in multiple divisions?" I kept firing questions at him as he got closer to me.

"No, that's..."

"Mad that I'm a girl and I'm better than you?"

Nate came right up to me and pushed me hard against the tree with his forearm.

"I gave you all the skills and we could've been a great pair!" he yelled right at me. "But then I saw you with Monahan and knew you were never interested in me at all!"

I was speechless and Nate backed away from me and lowered his voice. "I thought we had something between us and you chose him."

"Nate..." I started calmly.

"No, Lexi. He trained you, I can tell. He broke the rules and so did you. Neither one of you should be in the ORC," Nate answered quietly. "I acted rashly that night and took my anger out on you but it was really him I should have hurt."

I looked at him, puzzled by his words.

"What are you saying?" I asked.

"I was so mad at you when I saw you with him. You just used me to teach you what I knew and then you were just done with me!" Nate answered angrily.

"You and I were friends! We worked together to improve our skills, Nate!" I explained.

"You're wrong," he replied slowly and he turned away from me. "After I saw you with Monahan one of those last days, I knew you two were a thing. So I did what I had to for the ORC... I tried to get rid of you."

"You what?" I asked, dumbfounded.

"I started that fire in the cabin, Lexi! I orchestrated the entire thing!" Nate answered.

My mouth dropped open and I froze. There was just no way that Nate could have done that.

"I planned that entire evening out, knowing we were going to have some drinks with the other recruits and knowing the alcohol would incapacitate you. I waited too long to start the fire though since the other recruits were still awake. If I would've been quicker, you wouldn't have woken up and gotten out."

I was again speechless as I learned that Nate set the fire in our cabin, threatening both mine and Ally's lives out of jealousy and anger.

"You. Ass," I said through gritting my teeth. "Ally was in that cabin too, did you think about her!"

"She wasn't ever going to make it into the ORC. Collateral damage," Nate answered with a shrug.

"Collateral damage?" I shouted at him. "That's my sister! You better get on with it because if you don't, I swear, Nate..."

"What, Lexi? You'll do what? Absolutely nothing tied to a tree?" Nate smirked and let out a laugh.

I picked my feet up off the ground and pulled on the rope but it did nothing other than dig hard into my wrists. Nate chuckled again, knowing he had bested me and I felt my heart rate speed up as I began to panic.

I instinctively backed against the tree as Nate approached me but I had no where to go.

"Lexi!" a voice called in the distance. "Lexi! Where are you?"

Nate and I made eye contact as we both recognized Ally's voice calling for me. I looked to my right towards where the voice was coming from and opened my mouth to yell so Ally could hear where we were.

In the second that I looked away from Nate, he had closed the distance between us. He had also removed my thick medical tape from my bag and pressed a piece over my mouth.

He stood in front of me with his hands on my cheeks and pressed his thumbs over the tape that was keeping me silent.

"I will lead our team away from here and then come back to finish the job," he whispered to me. "Don't go anywhere now."

He took a step back but kept his hands on my face before he turned his back on me.

I tried to call out but the tape he used was medical-grade and was meant to be used on injuries and secure dressings tightly so it was working exceptionally well right now. I was left silent.

I stood on my toes and wrapped my hands around the rope and pulled up so I could lift one of my legs up and I kicked Nate in the back. It wasn't very strong but it caused him to stumble and from his kneeling position, he turned around and glared at me.

I stood on my right and shot my left leg out, trying to kick him with it but he grabbed it with his left hand and pushed back on me.

Faster than I could register, my backpack was on the ground and his fist was flying through the air again. I closed my eyes waiting for it to make contact with my face but it didn't. Instead, I felt his fist pressed against my thigh.

Less than a second later, the pain hit me.

It was excruciating and I felt my eyes instantly water. I looked down at Nate's fist on my thigh as he unclenched his fist and revealed the handle of my own knife sticking out of my thigh.

I tried to open my mouth to scream but with no success. Through the tears, I looked at Nate as he stood in front of me but not looking at me. He held his radio in his hand.

"Subject at marker 52, within 5 square miles," he whispered. He held the radio back up to his ear and chuckled as he lowered it back to his mouth. "She'll be here. She won't be going anywhere. Bring her body back to the Queen. Over and out."

He approached me again as we heard Ally call my name once more through the woods.

"Keep that still if you don't want to bleed out before I get back," Nate said and pointed at the knife sticking out of my leg. He put his hand around the handle and yanked it out of my leg.

If I could have, I would have screamed. The pain was unbearable as the steel sliced back out of my flesh and blood poured out of the wound and down my leg. It didn't matter if I moved or not, removing the knife would definitely cause me to bleed out, something that I was sure Nate knew.

I was crying and I wish I wasn't but the wound was pounding and I knew that I was in trouble. Darkness threatened to cloud my vision from the pain and I felt my vision swirling at the blood that was pumping out of the wound and down my leg.

I was barely able to see as Nate took the knife with my blood still on it and threw it into a nearby tree. He hung my backpack on it as he ducked off through the woods.

I closed my eyes to try to fight off the need to pass out from blood loss and I listened as Nate ran through the trees.

"Ally! Ally, is that you?" he called.

"Lexi? Oh. Nate, have you seen Lexi?" I heard Ally's voice full of worry.

"She went off on her own to find Cole," Nate said.

I heard Ally gasp. "Without anyone?"

"I followed her until I lost the trail but we need to find her before she gets hurt or lost. Wake everyone up, we have to go now," Nate said.

I started to lose focus and felt my body sagging against the tree I was leaning on. Blood was pooling on the roots under my feet and still running down my leg.

I didn't hear Nate or Ally anymore. The woods were quiet and I was alone.

I hung my head in defeat as I heard the distant sound of the engines starting from our caravan of vehicles and I knew that my team was running in the opposite direction in search of me even though I was right here.

I felt myself getting lightheaded from the loss of blood and the pain levels. I tried to breathe through my nose normally and distract myself from the pain but it wasn't working.

Tears continued to stream down my face as I leaned myself against the tree as my vision slipped sideways and I finally passed out.

7

I felt brightness trying to sneak in through my eyelids as my mind started to come to, but I held my eyelids shut although I felt them fluttering.

I had two thoughts on where I was and what was going on... and neither was great.

First, I died and this is the afterlife or whatever it's called now.

Second, I was still alive and Nate came back for me and I was about to be dead which brought me back to the first scenario anyway.

I decided I would open one eye and peek out to see what the end of my life looked like.

I was lying on my back and looked up to see it was daylight, the sun was out although it was hidden behind the trees above me, and I didn't think that I was dead. I could feel a slight breeze brush over my skin and I picked up my head to look around.

I immediately was hit with a wave of dizziness and so I laid myself back down but did notice that I had a pair of shorts on and my same t-shirt. I wasn't sure when I went from my tactical pants to shorts but someone must've saved me.

I came to this conclusion as the knife wound on my leg was wrapped up tightly with gauze and medical tape. I recognized it as the medical tape that Nate had used to keep me quiet and I felt fresh tears spring to my eyes as I vividly remembered what he did to me.

I pushed myself to a sitting position, ignoring the wave of dizziness and nausea that hit me when I did so, and held myself up and fought it.

It passed within a few minutes and I was able to sit up without the support of my arms. I was sitting on some sort of soft mat that I had previously been sleeping on and there was a small pillow my head had been resting on.

I put my hand on the side of my head where Nate had punched me and it was still tender, as was the front of my face where he hit me the second time after I overheard his conversation.

There was a pile of wet clothes next to the mat as well as... my backpack. I quickly grabbed it and opened it. Most of my things seemed to still be here although my knife was missing and so were some medical supplies although I couldn't recall exactly what.

I tucked my legs underneath myself and slowly stood up, favoring my uninjured leg over my right one. I let out a slow breath and put my right leg on the ground and took a step forward.

Surprisingly, it did not hurt. That must have meant I had been out for a while if it healed all the way to not hurt me when I walked.

I continued to take a few gingerly placed steps until I felt comfortable and began walking like I used to. I kept turning around to not go too far from the mat I woke up on so I could find my way back. If I was going to wander off, I wanted to take my bag with me.

I headed back towards the mat and scooped up my bag. As I turned around, I heard a rustling and some sticks snapping so I froze. I threw a quick look over my shoulder and eyed something I didn't notice before when I woke up.

There was a bow and quiver leaning against one of the trees. It was shiny and new so it must've been ORC issued, so there must be a Wielder from the ORC around. I grabbed it and I ducked behind one of the tree trunks I woke up near and stayed silent.

I calmed my breathing and willed my heart to stop pounding in my chest. If Nate emerged from anywhere, I was going to run for it. It didn't matter what direction or what I ran into, anything was better than being near him while having a target on my back.

I silently pulled an arrow from the quiver and I pulled the bow taut, holding the arrow and pointing the weapon at the ground.

"Dammit, where did she go?" a male voice whispered. I couldn't say for sure whether it was Nate as his whisper had no vocal timbre to recognize. I listened as they approached the mat and where I was. Their footsteps stopped and then turned around and headed away from me.

I slowly emerged from my hiding spot and stood between the two trees with my bow raised and pointed at the individual. I took another step out from behind the tree and my bare foot crunched on a leaf and the sound echoed throughout the air around us.

The man turned around and I got a look at his green and gray eyes. I pulled back slightly on my bow making sure it was taught and anchored my shot with my thumb on my cheek.

"Lexi..." Cole said to me as he slowly raised his hands.

I didn't move but let my eyes scan the scene in front of me, searching for Nate and whatever game he might be playing. Cole took a step towards me.

"Don't come any closer," I said and moved my aim right to the middle of his chest. "I won't miss."

My voice shook with fear, despite my attempt to hide it.

"Lexi, it's me," Cole said calmly. He stopped his advance but kept his hands up.

My brain was racing and I didn't know if I could trust him or not. He looked and sounded like Cole, but could this be some trick of Nate's? A psychological mind game before he took me out for good?

"Tell me something only Cole Monahan would know," I demanded.

Cole smiled a little bit and tipped his head back and looked up at the sky, thinking. "I could tell you what I got you for your birthday this year... because it's that back-pack that you're wearing."

I relaxed my arm a little bit but decided to still be wary because anyone could know that information... I think.

"Where did you take me on my birthday?" I asked.

Cole clasped his hands together on top of his head and rested them there.

"Phew, where didn't we go that day?" he said. "We rode into town. You drove, of course. I made a stop to get you a cupcake and we stopped to see Julianna. She gave you these sticky patches that you were really excited about and let me tell you... they work." He pointed down at my leg.

"You patched me up?" I asked.

He nodded and continued. "Anyway," he said, drawing out the beginning vowel, "then we rode to our place and ran into some of my... work colleagues." He smiled when he said that and I did too knowing he was referring to Damion, Wren, and DeLeo.

"I took a souvenir home from that day," I said, still holding my gaze and my weapon on him. "What was it?"

Cole scrunched his eyebrows but did not take his eyes off of me.

"Damion's pocket knife," he answered. "Any other questions, Lex?"

I kept my arrow taut on the bow but pointed it at the ground.

"How did you find me?" I asked.

Cole took a step towards me with his hands up and I didn't move. He took another one and I lowered my bow and arrow, indicating that I wouldn't shoot him.

After a few more steps, he was right in front of me. He put his hands on my hands and took the weapon from me and placed it on the ground next to us. He returned his hands to my hands and pulled me into a gentle hug.

I buried my face into his shirt as I hugged him back and began to cry. Cole rubbed circles on my back as I shook with tears.

"You're safe with me, Lex," Cole whispered and kissed the top of my head while keeping his strong arms around me.

He held me while I wept. I cried, knowing that *this* was Cole, *my* Cole, here with me. I cried, realizing that he didn't steal me from my life all those years ago, but rather he *saved me.* I cried, knowing that he just saved me again from whatever terrible fate Nate had planned for me. And finally, I cried with the understanding that I could never return home as long as I was breathing, now that Queen Camilla had ordered my death..

Cole led me back to the mat and we sat down together.

"How are you feeling?" he asked me. "Seems like the leg is pretty good."

"It feels fine," I answered. "You used the Restore on it?"

"That really sticky stuff? Yeah, it was just bleeding so much and I didn't know what else to do. You were so..." his voice trailed off and I placed my hands back in his.

"Thank you for saving me... again," I said.

"Lexi, when I found you in that clearing, I had assumed the worst. You barely had a pulse when I cut you down," Cole said. His voice cracked and threatened to betray his strong facade. "If I ever see Nate again…"

"Shh, Cole," I said and it was my turn to comfort him as I could see him beginning to shake with rage. "And I already made Nate a promise I'd kick his ass first for setting the fire."

Cole pulled back from me. "What? He set the cabin fire?" he asked.

"Sure did. He told me he planned the whole thing, down to getting me drunk, to eliminate me from the ORC. Turns out he's the jealous type and he didn't like our fraternizing," I explained.

"I knew I didn't like the way that kid looked at you," Cole said angrily.

"He had this radio to talk to Camilla with," I started. "She… um, admitted she started the fire when I was a child. So I know that… I know that it wasn't you. I'm sorry that I ever believed that it was."

"I understand, Lex," he answered. "I knew the second Camilla laid eyes on you, she would know exactly who you were, which is why Remy and I tried to hide you for so long. When she gave that order to Nate, I knew I had to come and find you."

"How did you know she gave Nate kill orders?" I asked skeptically.

Cole pulled a radio just like Nate's off of his waistband and showed it to me.

"I grabbed it when I was escaping so I could listen to their communications. It took me a few tries to find the right channel but once I did, I was able to listen in. Nate radioed for backup to come and pick you up where he left you so he could continue the mission to find me and I doubled back and got to you first," Cole explained.

Despite everything, I believed him. The pieces were starting to click together and the blank spaces were being filled in with the truth, as I pieced together my childhood and all of the secrets that my family kept from me.

"Cole?" I asked and looked at him. "Can you tell me how you got me out of the castle all those years ago?"

He smiled and pulled me closer.

"How much do you want to know?" he asked.

I looked him in the eyes and gave him my answer.

"Everything."

8

Cole's stories were enlightening as he spared no details and left nothing out. He began at the very beginning from overhearing the Queen's meeting with his own father and the old lady psychic to how we got to sitting here together in the forest somewhere outside of the kingdom.

Cole had said that I had been unconscious for a few days since he found me where Nate had left me but we had stayed in the vicinity. He had feared moving me too much while I was healing.

I was sitting at the edge of a small stream that cut through the wooded area. I had needed some space and time to process so I wandered off to clear my head. I selected a grassy spot where the warm sun was coming through the trees as it was getting lower in the sky.

I replayed Cole's tale again in my mind. Most of it I already knew, having lived it with him for the past fifteen years. It was those first few years of his story that were the most challenging to wrap my brain around. I felt like

I was living a secret life with Remy and Cole, but at the same time, maybe my royal life was the secret one.

I shook my head, unable to imagine myself growing up in that castle. I thought back to the day that Damion snuck me around and how large and lavish everything was. That could've been my normal.

But instead, I grew up in our little secluded cabin with Remy and Cole. I smiled at the thought and all of the memories I created with the two of them throughout the years.

A rustling behind me alerted me to Cole's approach and he sat down next to me and eyed my scars that were visible since I only had a t-shirt on before looking at the ground.

"That psychic should've told you it's rude to stare," I said jokingly. I had given Cole a look earlier when he told me about the psychic but he said that she was indeed a real person.

"She's called a visionary," Cole said again about the woman, "and I haven't seen her since that day."

"Well, what about your father?" I asked, also now understanding why Cole had never taken me to his house or introduced me to his father.

"I couldn't exactly ask him if he had seen her because then my secret would be out," Cole replied.

He tilted his head back to look up at the sky instead of at my exposed burn scars.

"I'm sorry I didn't get you out sooner. Perhaps the damage wouldn't have been as bad," he said to the sky.

I let out a small laugh. That brought his attention back to me with a confused expression on his face.

"Cole, if my options were living with these scars or... not living, don't you think I'd choose the first option?" I asked.

My question was rhetorical, so I was not surprised when he didn't answer.

"I've been thinking," I said.

"About?" Cole asked.

"All of it. Everything," I replied, running my hand up and down my arm, feeling the uneven terrain of my skin from that fire.

"My scars tell a story. They remind me that I am stronger than that fire, stronger than Camilla's actions and that I am still here," I said proudly.

Cole looked at me with a soft smile. He moved towards me, put his hand on my chin, and pressed his lips to mine gently.

I kissed him back before pulling away, feeling the fire in my cheeks.

"You are beautiful, Lexi," he said.

I blushed again and put my hands into the pockets of my torn shorts. Cole had told me he ripped my pants so he could treat my stab wound without undressing me.

I felt my hand brush against something in my pocket and pulled it out. It was a folded up piece of paper.

As I unfolded it, I remembered instantly it was the artwork from the frame in my bedroom that Remy had left for me. I quickly flattened it out and thrust it at Cole.

"Cole, do you know where this is? Remy left it for me," I explained.

He took it from me and analyzed the image, opening and closing his eyes several times like he was concentrating. Finally, when he opened them and didn't close them again, he handed me back the artwork.

"I can't say I'm familiar with it, but I wouldn't be surprised if Remy went there. Seems secluded. Any idea what type of supplies she took with her?" Cole responded.

"No, I'm sure she took her bike and whatever she could carry with her, but I didn't really look around. The ORC was tossing my house just fine without me," I said sadly.

I looked at Cole.

"Speaking of," I said with a smirk, "I heard that when you escaped, you took my bike."

Cole grinned.

"It better still be in one piece," I added and pointed my finger accusingly at him.

Cole shrugged and I gave him a little push. He nudged me back and I returned the favor. His next nudge tipped me over and we both laughed as he laid on the grass next to me, propping himself up on one of his strong arms.

Today his eyes were green and they looked between my own eyes and my mouth like he couldn't decide what to do. I gave him an approving head nod and he leaned in closer to me. He placed his other hand on the side of my head and was lowering himself towards me when the radio on his waistband crackled to life.

"Delta team, report!" it said.

I froze as I heard Nate's voice come out of the radio. I sat up immediately and thankfully Cole sensed my movement and rolled to the side so I didn't whack him in the head with my abrupt movement.

"I've been listening to them," Cole said. "They already searched the area I found you once, they probably are back looking for clues."

"No new tracks. She didn't return here... wait," the radio said in a voice that wasn't Nate's.

Cole and I also waited.

"Single tire treads here. She left on a bike," the radio said.

Cole and I exchanged looks and he grabbed my hands, pulling me to my feet.

"Time to go," he said to me and kept his hand in mine as we started running through the trees.

"Where?" I called as we ran.

"Anywhere the ORC reinforcements aren't showing up," Cole answered as he leaped over a fallen tree.

We came back to the area where I had woken up on the mat and he quickly rolled it up and flung it over his shoulder. He pointed at the bow and arrow which I threw over mine and my backpack over the other.

Cole took my hand and led me further through the trees. The low-hanging branches were rustling past me as we ran together further into the woods but I felt like I heard something else.

"Cole! Stop!" I said and yanked on his arm.

"Lexi, what?" he asked, panting.

I tilted my head up and closed my eyes, listening intently to the nature around me. I tuned out the leaves rustling, the birds chirping, and the slight trickle of that stream we found before and all that was left was near silence.

And the sounds of three bike engines in the distance but getting louder.

I opened my eyes to Cole looking at me quizzically.

"There's three of them, coming this way," I said.

"I don't hear a single thing," Cole answered looking around.

"Eyes open for Cole Monahan," Nate's voice crackled through the radio. "He also has an elimination order."

"Ah dammit," Cole said and ducked into some shrubs before wheeling my bike out towards me.

The purple stripe was gleaming down the side although the bike was rather dirty. It was covered in mud and honestly, probably some of my blood from where Cole had held onto me while driving me away from that terrible place.

Cole stopped the bike in front of me and tossed the mat into the storage compartment which I noticed was filled with several other shoulder bags and supplies. I was glad that he was prepared, unlike myself as I only had my backpack and whatever was left in it that Nate hadn't tossed out.

As soon as he shut the storage compartment under the seat, he hopped on and I joined him quickly, not waiting for an invitation. My feet rested right behind his and I had just wrapped an arm around his middle when he turned the throttle and we took off.

We sped over tree roots and uneven earth, trying to put as much distance between the ORC members and ourselves. The terrain made it difficult to go fast enough and before long, Cole could hear their engines too which meant they were definitely gaining on us.

"In pursuit!" the radio announced from Cole's waist.

I turned around and could see the three specks gaining on us through the trees.

"Cole!" I shouted.

"I'm going as fast as I can!" he shouted back.

The ORC was gaining on us quickly and as they got closer, I realized they had large, oversized tires that were meant for navigating difficult terrain like this. We had to go slow enough to ensure we didn't pop a tire or throw one of us off while they were able to plow through everything.

It had been risky for Cole to keep us so close to the site of where he rescued me from, but I understood that I wasn't stable at the time. I also know from experience how difficult it is to travel on a bike with an unconscious passenger. I was thankful he didn't leave me there to bleed out and I could only hope we made it out of this situation as well.

I turned around again and there were two ORC members approaching. I didn't see the third and I didn't want to find out where that one was so I urged Cole forward.

He made a hard right and I had to grip him with two hands so I didn't get thrown from the bike. There was a slight opening between two trees that was much too close for comfort but Cole squeezed us through it and the forest floor was much flatter here so we would be able to increase our speed.

The two bikes behind us had to navigate around the treeline as their tires made their bikes bigger and bulkier and unable to squeeze through the space that we did. But I knew they would catch us quickly, so I didn't get too excited.

"Duck!" Cole yelled.

I turned around to face the front and was hit with a force at my chest that threw me backward off of the bike and I landed on my back. I felt all the air knocked from my lungs at the impact and pressed my hand to my sternum where I had made contact.

I sat up and saw a thin rope running across the pathway at about my chest level. One end was tied to one tree and the other end was anchored into another tree from an arrow that was buried in it. I rubbed my head and then remembered what situation I was in and immediately pulled an arrow from behind me and I drew it back although I had no target to aim at.

I scanned the treeline for movement but didn't see any in front of me.

"Lexi!" Cole yelled as he turned the bike around and sped towards me. I turned and looked at him just in time to get tackled from behind.

I lost my arrow and flew into the ground face first. I put my hands out to stop myself as my back absorbed the weight of this ORC member laying on top of me. My hands were pinned under my own body and I couldn't get them free.

"Get off of her," Cole growled as he brandished a knife, my knife that was last used upon myself, and approached the ORC member.

"Cole Monahan," he said from above me at the sight of him. "You are under arrest." He picked up my bow and put an arrow in it and pointed it at Cole.

I shifted my weight hoping to throw off the guy's shot but surprisingly, he slid his weight off of me and I rolled sideways, quickly pulling my arms out from under me and turning to face him as he fiddled with the bow and arrow. He may have landed that one shot with the rope in the tree, but watching him now, he was clumsy with it, so I knew this was no Wielder.

I kicked him in the helmet and he tipped over, unmoving. I took back my bow and arrow and pointed it at him defensively as I approached him. Cole was by my side instantly.

"You okay?" he asked.

"Fine," I said, not taking my eyes off of the ORC member. "Take off his helmet."

Cole bent down and took off his helmet revealing a familiar face.

"Wren," I said, recognizing the blonde-haired guy I had once knocked out.

Suddenly Wren moved and grabbed my ankle. He tugged and pulled my body down and across his as Cole launched himself at Wren.

Wren moved sideways and wrapped his arm around my neck and although we were both sitting, he was taller than me and was effectively cutting off my air supply.

"Back up, Monahan," Wren said, "or I snap her neck right now."

I did not think Wren was bluffing by the amount of pressure he was exerting on my windpipe. I opened and closed my mouth like a fish trying to get air in but he was effectively cutting off my air supply.

"Wren, you're suffocating her," Cole said calmly after taking a few steps back.

I felt Wren release a little bit of pressure and I sucked in air hungrily. He held me with my back pressed up against his chest and my head to the side of his so that he could see Cole from where we were seated.

"Back up, Monahan," Wren repeated.

I pressed my hands into the grassy area we were sitting in trying to keep pressure off of my windpipe and I felt my fingers brush something hard and slick in the grass.

I realized it was one of my arrows, although we were both slightly sitting on it. I slowly traced my fingers along its smooth surface trying to get a grip on it. Once I wrapped my fingers around part of it, I threw my body to the right over the arrow knowing what Wren would do.

As I expected, he wrenched me to the left, picking us both up off of the arrow for less than a second. That was all the time I needed to pull the arrow out from under the weight of us and bring it down into his leg.

Wren let out a howl and let go of me as I scrambled to my feet. Cole reached for me and grabbed my arm, pulling me away from his Combatant teammate, or rather ex-teammate, who has held a grudge against me since the day I met him.

He pushed me behind him protectively and faced Wren who was now laying on his side and clutching his bleeding leg. I wasn't sure what he was going to do, but it wasn't like Wren was going anywhere. I could speak from experience how much an injury like that hurt.

"Let's go," Cole said to me and jogged towards where he left our bike.

I didn't follow him immediately, just looked at Wren and the damage and pain I had caused him. I was trying to justify my actions in my head but I couldn't.

I knelt down next to Wren and tore the sleeve off of his ORC tactical jacket.

"Lexi! Get away from him!" Cole yelled to me and came running back to my side.

He tried to pull me away but I shook him off as I tied the sleeve of the jacket above the stab wound. Wren cursed at me as I pulled it taut and took a swing at me but Cole pulled me back just in time.

"Don't pull the arrow out and keep that tourniquet on," I said to him.

"Don't think... this... is over, Probie," Wren managed through clenched teeth but he did not make any more moves. He groaned and remained on the ground and we moved away from him.

I whipped my head around at the sound of the approaching engines of the two remaining ORC members. I didn't want to stick around and see who they would be, in case they were as unfriendly and as loyal to the Queen as Wren was.

I pulled two arrows from my quiver and placed them both in my bow, sliding my middle finger between them to send them in opposite directions.

"Lexi!" Cole called. "What are you doing? We have to go!"

As the two bikes approached, I pressed my thumb to my cheek as Nate had taught me and exhaled. I maneuvered my middle finger to adjust the angle slightly and I let go, sending my arrows soaring at the two approaching ORC members.

I heard two unmistakable *pop! pop!* sounds and knew I hit my mark as the two bikes slowed and flopped to a halt with each of their front tires totally deflated.

I turned with my bow towards Wren's bike and then lowered my weapon and looked at Cole who looked at me approvingly.

"I'll follow you on this one," I said and hopped onto Wren's bike and twisted the throttle.

Cole was already mounting my bike, kicking the kickstand off the ground, and speeding off. I lifted my feet off the ground and let the bike pull me forward.

I turned around one last time to see the two remaining ORC members dismount their bikes and run towards their injured teammate before looking up at me as I followed Cole and sped away from them.

9

We drove and drove and drove.

I wasn't sure if we were ever going to stop but Cole was determined to put as much space between us and that ORC team.

Hours had gone by and we rode onward silently through the trees until we finally hit a real road we could follow. I wasn't sure where we were or where we were going and I bet Cole didn't know either, but the further from the ORC, the better.

I wasn't sure why I didn't feel guilty after my first meeting with Wren when I knocked him unconscious. But now, after thrusting an arrow into his leg, I felt awful. My stomach was still in knots.

Perhaps I was like Remy. As a doctor, she had a moral compass that guided her to do no harm and to help people. I felt similarly but felt like I had violated this unspoken code by stabbing Wren. I had been wrestling with the concept that it was either me dying by asphyxiation or me stabbing him so I didn't die. I was about ninety percent sure that the wound wouldn't kill him either, especially since I put a tourniquet on it and told him not to remove the arrow, unlike what Nate did to me.

I shuddered thinking of him again. I froze earlier when I heard his voice come out of Cole's radio, meaning that I let Nate successfully get inside my head. Just the thought of him paralyzed me with fear.

I almost didn't notice Cole slowing down in front of me, but I heard his engine start to slow as he let go of the throttle.

It was dark out, late in the night and it would have been challenging to see without the lights on our bikes, even with my impeccable eyesight.

I stifled a yawn as Cole stopped his bike and dismounted.

"I think we've covered enough ground for now," Cole said, rubbing the sleep from his eyes. "Why don't you get set up to rest and I'll take the first watch?"

I dismounted from my big ORC bike and crossed the space to Cole.

"Cole, we are both exhausted and neither one of us will last more than five minutes," I answered. "Let's both sleep and just keep each other safe."

Cole opened his mouth and let out a huge yawn as I said that and we both chuckled.

"I guess you're right," he said. He put his hands on my arms which were still bare and looked me up and down. "Geez, Lex, you're freezing. Let's see what we have here to warm you up," he added as he opened up the storage compartment in Wren's ORC bike.

He dug around for a bit and pulled out Wren-sized ORC gear and tossed it to me. I pulled the pants on over my shorts and zipped up his combatant jacket with its blue embroidery on the sleeve. Even though it was several sizes too big for me, I was instantly warmer.

"He has a sleeping bag in here so let's use that," Cole said, pulling the sleeping bag out of the compartment.

I stood back while he unrolled it and laid it next to the sleeping mat I had used the previous few nights. Without the sun and the adrenaline, I felt the chill of the night air.

"Here, Lex," Cole said. "You take the sleeping bag and I'll sleep next to you on the mat."

I followed his orders and climbed into the sleeping bag. It was definitely warmer in there but I felt the coldness from the ground seeping through the bottom as Cole settled next to me.

With the sleeping bag pulled up around my chin, I turned to Cole although his eyes were already closed and I could see occasional shivers wrack his upper body.

"Cole?" I asked.

He opened one eye and looked at me.

"I... um, I was thinking," I started. I realized how awkward I sounded. I was going to suggest that he and I share the sleeping bag in order to get closer together and warm up with each other's body heat. It's not like I just wanted him close to me. Okay, maybe I did, but I was doing it in the name of survival.

It hadn't been that long since Cole told me that he loved me right before Camilla had him hauled off to prison for my alleged kidnapping. Although I had mixed feelings when starting out this mission with my team, who had also abandoned me and trusted Nate, I knew my feelings were true for Cole. This was all so new to me still and I didn't want to come off as inexperienced... even though I was. But then I remembered this was Cole, and he's seen me at my best and my worst, which was probably fairly recently when I almost bled to death.

"Lex?" he asked, still peering at me through that one opened eye.

If I could join the ORC, and wanted to continue to survive with those kill orders out there against me, I needed to change my attitude and start exuding more confidence and less fear. I took a deep breath before I spoke and looked Cole in the eyes... or rather eye.

"Let's put this sleeping bag on the mat to keep the cold out, and we can share it so we both stay warm," I said confidently.

Cole opened his other eye and looked at me.

"Are you sure?" he asked.

"Positive," I said, just adding to the strength of my decision.

In one movement, Cole jumped up and pulled the sleeping bag with my body in it over onto the mat, and slid himself inside right next to me. I could instantly feel the warmth of him next to me as he wrapped an arm protectively around my middle, pulling me close to him.

I could feel the increase in his heartbeat with his chest pressed against my back. I felt my heartbeat pick up as well at the close proximity. No matter how hard I tried, I could not squash the feelings he gave me when he was near, or when I thought about him.

While I was secretly terrified about what lay ahead, I knew that having Cole near me was helping quell some of my fears. The constant threat that Nate, my mother, and the entirety of the ORC were hunting for me (and Cole, too), not to bring us in alive and well, but rather to eliminate us by whatever means necessary was terrifying. The fact that Damion and Ally were out searching for me *with* Nate, who could harm them at any time, was also in the back of my mind. The only thing that helped ease my thoughts was that I knew Camilla loved them and probably wouldn't want them harmed, although she had no problem using Ally as leverage against me. Surely, she had known I would do anything to keep my sister safe.

I felt Cole's breathing even out as he fell into a much-needed sleep tucked against me. But my mind continued to race.

I was glad that I found him, or rather that he found me and saved my life... again. But I was determined to find Remy too. It wasn't fair for her to be punished and have to flee because of me. I decided that in the morning, we would set out to find this mountain range where I assumed Remy would be hiding.

I was aware that this would not be easy. It was quite literally a mountain of a task trying to search for her in a place where I had never been. Up until a few days ago when I left the kingdom limits with Damion in the jeep, I had never left home. It wasn't even until ORC training that I had left the comfort of my home with Remy.

But what would happen once we were reunited, *if* we were reunited? It's not like we could go back to our cabin in the woods as it would be too dangerous for any of us to return to Odessa.

It was sinking in that I would never get to return to my home and as long as Camilla was in power, Cole and I would always be on the run.

But at least he and I were together.

Hopefully, that would last longer than the nervous pit in my stomach indicated.

10

Cole and I fell into a routine over the next week or so as we continued to travel onward. Every day when we got up, one of us would scout the perimeter and then we would pack up and keep moving.

I was thankful that Remy had thought ahead and packed some of my clothes in the storage compartment of my bike the day that I left with Ally, so I was fortunate to have clothes that actually fit. As we drove on our separate bikes, we looked for any sign of mountains, any sign of tracks, and any sign of people, but were met with nothing except for more forest. In addition, the radio that Cole stole was silent indicating that we were largely alone out here.

The greenery was lovely, and we were able to find fresh water sources often enough, but all we did was eat, travel, rest and repeat. I had hoped we would have found something, passed a town or anything but unfortunately, we didn't.

We didn't cover a lot of ground since we only traveled during the daytime and the bikes didn't go too fast. But it was enough to be away from the ORC… and Nate.

Cole was good company, though.

We did some training exercises and I tried to teach him to wield the bow but he was disastrous with it. We would race and I still lost every time to Cole's large stride, but in our combat matches, I put up a fair fight, being lighter and more agile than he was.

We relived our adventures as kids growing up with Remy and he told me more about his life. He told me numerous times that he never once regretted saving my life when we were kids, but always regretted not telling me who I was. Regardless, I've been thankful every day that I grew up the way that I did.

"Would've been nice to eat off of fancy dishes like you did," I said jokingly.

"Only when my father and I were invited to fancy dinners," he had answered. "And only when I was older."

He told me how hard it was to watch Damion mourn, knowing that I was well and alive. He told me how Allyson basically disappeared after the fire that took her twin and that the next time he really saw her was at the ORC training.

We stopped for a break as dusk fell and I climbed off my bike and stood next to Cole and took his hand.

"I have no regrets," I said, looking him in the eyes.

"I know you don't," he replied.

"And you shouldn't, either," I added. I pushed myself up onto my toes and gave him a gentle kiss, sending butterflies to my stomach. "Don't let this eat away at you."

I walked away to establish a perimeter and left him with his thoughts for a moment. I knew things were bothering him and I wanted to make him feel better. I had made peace with all of his choices and my own choices, deciding that the good outweighed the bad every single time.

It was getting darker out and soon the only light would be from the moon so I wanted to move quickly and not lose Cole in the trees at night. I was halfway through my perimeter when I heard a loud popping sound that startled me, causing me to freeze.

Suddenly the sky was full of color and the forest around me lit up to the sound of these pops. The lights pulled my eyes to the dark sky.

"Lexi!" Cole called and I heard his feet pounding the earth.

"Over here!" I answered and pushed myself away from Cole's voice and towards the lights. "Cole, come here!"

I broke through the trees and found myself overlooking a city. A huge city. My eyes followed the trail of light to the sky as fireworks burst against the dark background of the night sky.

"Oh thank goodness," Cole huffed as he arrived at my side and his eyes followed mine to the display of lights.

We stood in silence as the fireworks went off, lighting up the sky in all different colors. The embers cascaded down from where they burst, like a rainbow waterfall above us.

"Cole, look," I said, taking my eyes off of the sky and pointing to the town below, more specifically the castle and the scenic background that lay behind it. I pulled out the folded painting from my pocket and held it up in comparison.

"The mountain peaks are similar, just backwards," Cole said as he pointed from the painting to the mountain range in the distance.

"So we need to see them from the other side," I concluded, "and we might find Remy."

"Get a look at this kingdom, it's got to be double the size of Odessa," Cole said, letting out a low whistle.

"We just have to get through it to the mountain range on the other side," I answered confidently.

"We should be careful," Cole replied. "Maybe go around in case they aren't friendly."

I thought about it for a moment, considering the fireworks. Fireworks implied a celebration of sorts. "Who has fireworks and isn't friendly?" I asked innocently.

Cole smiled and rolled his eyes at me.

"We can get a closer look now using the cover of nightfall and decide what the best option will be, okay?" he asked.

I gave him a smile and a nod.

"What about the bikes?" I asked.

"I had just finished hiding them when I heard the first fireworks so they'll be okay until we come back," he explained.

We looked each other over and were both wearing mostly all-black clothing. The goal was to not be noticed and observe so hopefully we'd blend in and not be spotted. The only weapon I was bringing was my knife which was already in my ankle holster and tucked under my pants and out of sight. I thought carrying a quiver over my shoulder and a bow might make me stick out.

Cole and I carefully slid down the hillside that we had been standing on and jogged towards the town, trying to keep low as the fireworks continued to burst above our heads.

We came to the first structures that signaled the outskirts of the city before the open land and the forest we had been hiding out in. It looked similar to our small town of Odessa and I could see people milling about, shops and storefronts up ahead.

"There's not going to be anywhere to hide," I whispered, pointing to the streets ahead. We would be on an open street and everyone could spot us. "Should we go back?"

Cole looked at where I was pointing and shook his head. I watched his eyes as they watched the people who passed by further up the road. There was a couple and the woman had her arm looped through the man's as they laughed and pointed up at the sky. When I looked back at Cole, he was looking at me with his arm out towards me.

"Seems like the best way to blend in," he said as I took his hand. He let me rest my other hand on his forearm as he guided us into this unknown place.

My head swiveled back and forth as I surveyed for danger, but also was taking in the various storefronts. There were so many shops that sold foods, cakes, sweets, bread, and more with scents that filled my nostrils, made my mouth water and my stomach rumble.

It occurred to me that Cole and I had basically only eaten a few nutrition bars a day for who knows how long and that was it The aromas of freshly baked goodies called to me.

"Sir, would you and your lady like to try the pound cake?" a gentleman asked from one of the shops.

"Oh, no thank you, sir," Cole replied to the gentleman holding a tray full of cakes and continued walking.

I, however, stopped at the delicious smell of the cake and Cole pulled on my arm but I stayed rooted to the spot.

The gentleman who offered the cake chuckled as I looked in his shop's window. He put one of the cakes on a square paper napkin and handed it to Cole.

"Have a free sample for your lady and enjoy your evening," he said with a smile.

"Thank you!" I said excitedly as Cole handed me the cake and then a little more firmly pulled me forward. We did have a purpose for being here after all, and it wasn't for snacks.

I took a small bite of the pound cake. It was warm and moist and the most delicious cake I had ever tasted. I heard Cole snort from next to me and I looked up at him as I continued to devour the treat.

"You have crumbs all over your face," he said with a laugh.

"Cole, this cake is so good. Try it!" I answered.

He smiled at me and shook his head, letting me finish the cake in peace.

We continued our way up the street acquiring various other snacks on the way, in addition to a flower that someone gave Cole which he also handed to me. This town seemed nice and maybe if Cole and I had to live somewhere new, we could settle here in this one, which I learned from one of the store owners was called Middletown.

The name was foreign to me and I also thought it a little strange but people from the outside probably thought that the name Odessa, where we were from, was also a little strange too.

"It seems like we could blend in here if we needed to," Cole said to me as we continued to walk.

"I was thinking that too," I answered. "But these streets are too narrow for transportation so if we were on our bikes, we'd probably have to go around the town."

"I haven't seen any transportation actually, have you?" Cole asked.

He was right. I shook my head no.

The streets started to feel a little more crowded as people seemed to be heading in the same direction we were, which was towards the expansive castle and the source of the fireworks.

"Let's head that way," Cole said and pulled me down a side street that was less populated. We crossed over a few more streets until we were the only people. "We should head back," he added and he nodded back in the general direction of the forest we had come from.

"Where do you think everyone is going?" I asked.

"Maybe towards the castle?" Cole guessed with a shrug. "Not sure what is going on there but I assume the fewer people we are around, the better."

"And where do you think you're going?" a voice asked from behind us.

Cole and I spun quickly and he tightened his grip on my hand. A lone figure stood in the middle of the street about five feet from us, dressed in dark colors much like we were. His hood was up and when we turned to face him, he brushed it back, revealing his face.

It was a tall man and he was similarly built to Cole, meaning he probably wouldn't be easy to take down but between the two of us, I didn't anticipate it being too much of a problem if it came to it. His face was rather square and his pointed chin stuck out at us.

"I asked you a question, newbie," the man said, looking at Cole and taking a step towards us. Cole protectively took a side step putting himself mostly in front of me. A sweet gesture every time but he knew that I could take care of myself.

A low whistle from behind us caused me to turn around in the direction we wanted to head in as two more men joined us, their feet crunching on the rocky path we were standing on. Their attire was the same as the first guy who stopped us.

"One of the newbies already found himself a lady?" one of the men behind me asked and he whistled low again.

When I turned back around, the first guy was only a foot away from us now.

"What do you want?" Cole asked, keeping his voice low and threatening.

I watched as the stranger's eyes moved from Cole's face to me, as I was peering out from beside Cole.

"Who's that?" he asked, pointing at me.

"None of your business," Cole answered.

The man smiled at me then flicked his eyes back to Cole, and the smile disappeared from his face. "Then I suggest you come back with us quietly, we won't tell the big guys and she can go back to wherever she came from," he said.

One of the guys behind us grabbed my arm and yanked me back and away from Cole. The movement was so sudden and unexpected that I let out a little shout.

I got my bearings quickly and drove my elbow into the man's face as he pulled me back. I felt and heard the crack of his nose as I made contact. He let go of my arm and I spun away from him and backed against a wall.

I looked up to see the first guy looking at me, Cole looking at me, the guy I hit bleeding on the ground, and the other guy with a weapon out and trained on me. It looked like one of the paint weapons that the ORC used but it was much smaller and the man held it in one hand.

"Put the gun down and I'll come with you," Cole said, not taking his eyes off of me.

Gun? We never used actual guns in the ORC. They caused damage and destruction and I didn't want to try to find out what fired out of this one that was pointed right at me.

"Let's go," the man said and pushed Cole in the direction away from me. "I hate having to round up the new ones."

Cole turned around and looked back at me, giving me a look that said he would be okay as he went with the first man and the guy with the broken nose. The other guy stayed behind with his weapon still trained on me.

"Go home," he finally said to me. He clicked something on his weapon, tucked it away, and then ran in the direction that the other two went in.

I stayed leaning against the wall and let out a breath.

"So much for anything being easy," I said out loud but mostly to myself. I looked in the direction that those three men had taken Cole and knew I wasn't going to just leave him behind.

I took off running after them, making sure to keep my footsteps light. I was running based on intuition and which way I thought that they would be heading, which I assumed was the direction of the castle. It didn't take me long to catch up to them because once the guy with the weapon caught up to them, they were all just walking.

I stayed a good amount back from them and ducked in and out of other streets to avoid being spotted. Pressing up against buildings covered me in a layer of dirt and dust but it didn't matter to me. I had to help Cole escape and then the two of us could run... again. I felt guilty for convincing him to let us explore the inside of this city and now he was being taken somewhere by strangers and I was on my own.

Finally, the castle came into sight and as I paused at the corner of a shop, I could see Cole walking with the three guys as they headed down a hill towards the open fields to the right of the castle. I couldn't go much closer without them seeing me so I stayed where I was and just watched to see where they went.

It was hard to see as they descended down the incline, but I kept my eyes on them as long as I could until they were out of sight. I ran out from my spot and followed them, hoping I would catch up with them but by the time I got down the hill, they were gone.

I stood in a gardened area, much like the one that was outside of the castle at home, looking around trying to figure out where they took Cole. I must've spun myself in several circles before a quiet voice stopped me from spinning.

"Are you lost?" the voice asked.

I stopped, tensed, and faced the girl who spoke. She was small, probably close to my age, just petite, and dressed in a very plain light blue dress. Her light brown hair was up in a neat bun with a light blue ribbon that matched the dress.

I stared at her and offered no answer, trying to decide if I should run or not.

She took a step closer to me. "I'm Ellis," she said and stuck her hand out towards me. "You must be the new castle staff they sent to join us."

"You work in the castle?" I asked her.

She nodded and gestured to her dress. "I know, it's deceiving but this is the work uniform here so that we always look nice."

I decided at that moment I was going to seize this opportunity and run with it. If I had to pretend to work in the castle to get full access to it and hopefully find Cole wherever they took him, then I was going to do it.

"I'm Lexi," I answered and shook Ellis' hand. "Sorry, I got lost."

Ellis smiled at me.

"Surely you just followed the fireworks for Prince Joseph's birthday to get here!" she said excitedly. "Most people don't know where to go when they get here."

"I, um... saw a few other people walking this way," I said, trying to sound innocent.

"Oh, probably some of the Middletown Army guys heading over to the Lodge," Ellis explained. "Good thing you didn't follow them!"

"What's the Lodge?" I asked.

"That's where the army guys stay and train and do whatever it is they do over there. Recruiting, fighting, it's dumb. Most of those guys are meatheads anyway. It's just behind the castle, here," she said.

I chuckled a little at the word "meathead," having never used it in conversation before. I assumed it didn't have a good meaning based on the way that Ellis used it.

"Well, let's get you inside and cleaned up, Lexi," Ellis said and waved me to follow her as she turned around and headed into the castle.

"This is the staff entrance," she said as we walked inside. "The Royal Family is almost never down here so this is where we come and go. I mean, you can go anywhere in the castle and will probably be summoned anywhere but this is like our home base. Our kitchen is here, we have a living room of sorts, it's just nice to have our own space, you know?"

It was set up like a typical house with a hallway running down the middle and there was indeed a kitchen taking up one side, and a living room with couches and tables and chairs on the other side. Everything was clean, white, gray, and light blue themed. It was relaxing to look at.

We continued down the long hallway and we left the large open rooms behind. This next portion of the hallway had more hallways heading to the left and the right and was full of closed doors.

"These are our sleeping quarters. Everyone gets their own room, which is very courteous of the Royals to allow us that luxury. Let me show you to yours," Ellis said as we moved along.

I wasn't sure how I was going to keep everything straight, but I wouldn't be here long so it wasn't too important. Thankfully, the room Ellis took me to was in the main hallway and was the second to last door before the double doors at the end.

She opened the door and gestured me inside. The room was small, probably comparable to my room back home with Remy. It had a bed in the middle against the back wall, with a nightstand on each side, a dresser, and one door on each wall which I assumed were closets. It was a nice space and would be a nice change from sleeping on the ground these past few weeks.

"Closet and your own bathroom," Ellis said, pointing at the door on the left and then on the right.

I had half-correctly assumed that those doors were closets since one was and the other was a bathroom... my own bathroom. Such luxury!

"It's nice that you're down here on the end with me," Ellis said. "I'm the last room before those double doors you saw, which take you into the main castle."

"Thanks for the mini tour," I said. I was hesitant to try my luck by asking for what I really wanted. I felt like Ellis wouldn't catch on though. "Can you show me the Lodge?"

"Do you really want to see it?" Ellis asked, tipping her head sideways at me.

"Just so I know where it is and how to avoid it," I answered quickly.

Ellis let out a huff of air.

"Phew, that's a great idea. Can't have you stumbling over there by mistake. They'd eat you alive!" she said with a laugh. "Come with me."

We exited my new sleeping quarters and left the way we came back to the outside world.

"Are they that scary?" I asked, trying to sound concerned.

"The army is all guys, always trying to prove themselves tougher than the next guy, you know? They are always training, running, staying fit, which isn't terrible, if you know what I'm saying," Ellis said, nudging me in the side with a laugh while we walked. "They sometimes mess with the new staff here, so just be alert. We mostly just bring their uniforms over or supplies from the castle if they need it but usually they don't need or ask for much."

"What are they training for?" I asked. We were heading through the garden I stood in before and crossing to the opposite side. Ellis held a gate open for me and I followed her through it.

"Nothing. Everything. Who knows? All I do know is that they just keep the kingdom safe, especially now," Ellis answered.

"Especially now?" I inquired. We walked past a barn-like structure and I could see through the open sliding door that it was filled with hay. I was interested to know if any animals lived here.

"I overheard a few of the guys talking the other day that two criminals escaped from another kingdom and are on the loose!" Ellis answered. Her blue eyes got wide when she answered and looked at me. "Can you imagine if they came here!"

My eyes got equally as wide as hers but for different reasons than whatever emotion she was feeling. I guess word had quickly spread that Cole and I were now fugitives and it was dumb luck that our pictures and names weren't plastered everywhere. I realized that I hadn't answered Ellis for a while and I had to cover for myself.

"Well, two criminals probably don't stand a chance against the army," I said quickly.

"Mhm," Ellis said with a nod and stopped walking. "Well, the Lodge is through there." She pointed to a large wooded area ahead of us. "It's a structure that looks kind of like a big house and on both sides has these smaller structures, which is where the army members sleep."

It seemed comparable to where we trained in the ORC. It was a logical setup for sleeping, eating, training, and keeping people together. I couldn't tell from here if they had any security measures in place, which would add to my challenge of getting inside and getting Cole out.

I was remembering our encounter with those three army men who took Cole. Now that Ellis had told me that only men were in the army, I know why they took him and not me, but I wondered why they thought he was a recruit.

"Hey Ellis, how does the army recruit?" I asked.

"Men who are older than twenty-one are recruited. You serve your three years and then you can leave and go into the reserves, so they'll come get you if they really need you or you serve your three years and still stay and continue to be in the army," she explained.

I regarded her explanation as she continued. "Prince Joseph turned twenty-one today, so I assume he will join the army and probably be a leader. We should go, the new recruits tend to sneak out when big events happen and I wouldn't want to be them when the trainers find them sneaking around the celebration."

"You sure know a lot about it," I said, eyeing her.

She didn't react to my statement, just shrugged her shoulders and turned around to head back.

"Come on, let's head in. I'll be with you tomorrow since it's your first day but we should get some rest," Ellis said.

I turned to look again towards the Lodge and wondered where Cole was and what he was doing right now. I let a small smile spread across my face knowing that whatever situation Cole was in, he was handling it. He was the best Combatant that I knew and he could take care of himself.

"Coming, Lexi?" Ellis called. I hadn't realized she had already put some distance between us.

"Coming!" I answered and hurried after her, ready to get some needed rest before figuring out how to infiltrate this kingdom's army in the morning.

11

I hadn't slept this well since Damion let me sleep in his guest room before the ORC training began. That was all before I knew that he was my brother, that I also had a twin sister and a monster of a mother who was hell-bent on destroying me, simply because an old, psychic woman told her that I was going to destroy her first.

I took a quick shower, which was refreshing after not having a real shower since being on the run. The water wasn't too hot but I wasn't going to complain. It was running water and wasn't me washing myself off in a river somewhere so I was going to take it and be thankful. I hoped that Cole had living quarters comparable to these for his time here in Middletown.

I opened the closet and it was empty, so I opened a few of the drawers in the dresser until I found something to wear. I pulled out a pair of tight black shorts and pulled them on. They were fitted and snug but I didn't mind. They were pretty short too. Short enough that the thin scar left behind from Nate's stab wound was visible.

Thankfully, Cole had used my Restore medication to seal that wound and make the scar minimal. It wasn't like I needed another scar anyway.

I opened another drawer that had a pullover sweatshirt that I put on. It was a little big but comfy nonetheless.

I wasn't sure what to do next while I waited for Ellis to wake up and come retrieve me so I wandered out of my little room and to the kitchen area she had shown me yesterday. I decided that it was time for me to have a proper meal besides the bars that Cole and I had been surviving on and the sweets I was handed in the town last night. I opened and closed every cabinet surveying what we had in terms of cookware and food.

The cabinets contained an impressive variety of snacks and ingredients. I decided to play it safe and put some cereal in a bowl with some milk. I sat on one of the stools in the kitchen and ate my cereal in silence. I was just about done when Ellis appeared in the kitchen.

"There you are!" she said when seeing me perched on the stool. "You weren't in your room." I spooned the last bite into my mouth and moved to wash my dishes as she continued. "I got you a few uniforms. Hopefully, they're the right size for you."

She held up three of those light blue dresses on hangers for me, each with a ribbon tied around the hanger.

I had not worn a dress in years. I couldn't even remember the last time that I had put one on. I remembered finding the box in my basement with the pieces of my purple dress from the fire. That was likely the last time I ever wore a dress.

I felt tears prick at the backs of my eyes at the painful memory, took the dresses from Ellis and headed to my room, saying a quick thank you as I went past her.

I managed to keep the tears in and willed myself to be strong. I made it out of that fire and out of that life into this new life that Cole and Remy had helped me to create.

I pulled on the dress, keeping my shorts on for added comfort. They were snug enough that they wouldn't make the dress look bulky and you couldn't see them. I took the ribbon and tied it around the end of my braid, hoping that would be enough to please Ellis rather than putting my hair up in a bun. I spun around to give myself a look and I stopped.

The short sleeves of the dress barely went past my shoulders and I could see my scars clear as day on the backs of my arms. The worst of it was on my back so thankfully the dress went high enough to hide that but not my arms. Ellis hadn't given me a sweater or anything and I wasn't sure I would be allowed to wear my jacket, especially with it being so dirty.

There was a light knock at my door. I felt the tears threaten to fall again so I looked up and fanned my eyes trying to keep them inside. I tried to remind myself that no one here knew who I was and no one knew of my past and what had caused those scars. I thought I could start over here, but not if everyone knew me as the girl with all of the scars.

Cole told me that they were beautiful and I was beautiful, but as I ran my hands over the slight texture on my arms, I was filled with sadness. They reminded me that although I survived, my own mother was the cause of them. She did this to me, she labeled me as a fugitive and she still wanted me dead.

I put my arms down and turned to answer the door. But when I spun around, I found Ellis standing in my room, right behind me. She put her arms unexpectedly around me while mine were still at my sides and gave me a hug.

"You shouldn't cry over that, Lexi," Ellis said to me while she still hugged me. "Those scars show that what-ever you went up against didn't win, you did. Because you're still standing here."

She pulled back from me and I looked at her and her eyes were shiny too. She rolled up her dress to expose the top of her leg and I saw a thick, raised line about five or six inches across. She, too, had a scar in a similar spot to where Nate gave me mine.

"You aren't the only one with scars, and you should embrace it," she said to me as she rolled down her dress and smoothed it out.

While my burns took up most of my back and my arms, that scar on her leg was long and angry. It looked like it was not done by a medical professional and the edges barely healed appropriately. I was curious about Ellis' tale, but I didn't think this was the right time.

I looked over my shoulder at the mirror and at my scars.

"I'm sure the people that love you don't see your scars. I'm sure they only see you," Ellis said as she walked to the door of my room and nodded. "Let's go take a grand tour."

I let out a breath and followed her, my arms and shoulders exposed as I left the safety of my bedroom. We pushed through the double doors and into the main part of the castle, where the color scheme was much darker than our quarters, the floor was carpeted and the walls were paneled with cherry-colored wood.

I heard noise and commotion up ahead and we rounded the corner as Ellis pushed us through two swinging silver doors. This must be the real kitchen where the serious cooking happens.

"Chefs, give a hello to Lexi, our new staff," Ellis said to the chefs in white who were swiftly moving around.

A rousing chorus of hello's and welcome's sounded from the group and Ellis let the silver doors swing shut as we left the kitchen. She pointed out various other rooms such as offices, study areas, a dining room, and then we ascended a few steps and came to a large and spacious open area.

It was similarly designed to the great room in our castle back home but this one had two staircases that came from each side and met in the middle before coming down into the center of the room. The floors were made of beautiful wood and the room was full of tall windows which looked out over the kingdom.

"Wow. This is lovely," I said out loud and my voice echoed off the walls. I quickly covered my mouth with my hand but my voice had already carried.

"I'm so sorry, Ellis," I whispered to her as she smiled.

"It's okay!" she said quietly and her voice didn't carry. "I'm sure there's no one around."

"Miss Ellis!" someone called from behind us.

We both turned around as a nicely dressed man was descending the staircase and heading towards us. He was wearing brown pants, a pressed white buttoned shirt, and fancy shoes. Whoever he was, he dressed like he was important.

"Dammit," Ellis whispered. "Follow my lead."

The handsome older man swooped down the stairs and approached us with a bit of a lilt in his step.

"Your Majesty," Ellis said and bowed her head to the man as he stopped in front of us.

Oh yes, definitely important. This had to be the King.

Following her lead, I bowed my head slightly at the King's arrival. So much for no one being around.

"Miss Ellis, how are you, dear?" the King asked.

"Fine, thank you, sir," she answered with a smile. "This is Lexi, a new addition to our staff."

"Excellent. How do you do, Miss Lexi?" the King asked me and stuck out his hand.

I stepped towards him and shook his hand. "I'm well, sir, thank you. It's nice to meet you" I answered, plastering a smile on my face.

"Firm handshake, dear. You've surely impressed a person or two before, I am sure," he answered.

"Thank you, sir," I said, dropping his hand. I folded my hands together in front of me as the king regarded us before taking a step back.

"Do enjoy your day and welcome to our home, Miss Lexi. I look forward to seeing you around," the King replied before giving us both a nod and walking off down a hallway. His long stride had him out of our sight in less than ten paces.

I turned to look at Ellis, and she was looking at me and struggling to hold in a laugh.

"What?" I asked her.

The laugh burst from her lips and filled the great room with its sound.

"I can't believe... of all people," she managed to get out between laughs. "I had just said that no one was around and of course, *of course*, it was King Joseph."

"He seems nice," I offered, still not finding it as hilarious as Ellis did. She was currently wiping tears from her eyes.

"Oh, he is very nice. Always says hello and doesn't want much. You handled yourself really well back there in front of him. Most people would panic," Ellis said.

"I am good with people," I said lamely. "I can talk to anyone about nearly anything." While it was a lame excuse, it was true. I didn't have many problems talking to people, even strangers. I wasn't about to offer the information to Ellis that royalty didn't intimidate me, except for perhaps my mother who had her own army at her command, currently hunting Cole and I.

"I'll say. I was afraid you might've made a fool of yourself but I was impressed."

I took the half compliment silently and let Ellis lead me onward. She took us up those mirrored staircases to the second floor which housed some of the royal family and also several guest rooms.

She explained that I would spend some of my time here, straightening up the rooms and making sure the rooms, bathrooms, and closets were all stocked appropriately with linens. The way Ellis explained everything, I learned that she was very proud of her work here and she said she would hold me to high standards as well.

I wasn't too worried about meeting her standards.

The job wasn't going to be physically draining, perhaps mentally draining, trying to remember everything all while keeping a smile plastered on my face and also remembering that I was in a dress. I was already planning on how to complete all of my tasks and then sneak out at night to the Lodge to find Cole to get him and I out of here.

"Any questions about which room is which?" Ellis asked and I snapped back to life.

I looked at her with wide eyes, realizing I had not been paying attention one bit and she gave me a small smile.

"I know it's overwhelming. I used a map when I first started, so I can draw one out for you," she said.

"That would be helpful, thanks," I answered, grateful that Ellis was kind and patient.

She walked me along a hallway that had full-length windows on one side which she said opened up to a balcony. She pushed aside the curtain and opened one so that I could see and she and I stepped out into the fresh air.

We were overlooking the Lodge and could see the small figures moving around their main building below. I was glad to finally get a glimpse of it now that I had a higher vantage point. The figures were moving quickly and all seemed to be carrying boxes and heading towards an open field.

"What are they doing?" I asked her.

"Not sure exactly, but it's some sort of competition to see who gets to be the rank leaders of the army," Ellis answered. "It changes every year but usually the same people take the roles. This year will be interesting because the Prince is eligible and the King wants him to be one of the leaders, naturally."

I thought for a moment as I watched the army members move around like small ants. The King didn't strike me as that type of person, but then again, neither did Queen Camilla when I first met her and watched her embrace her children with such love.

I wondered if Cole would stick to the shadows or try to prove himself. He never backed away from a challenge, so it was questionable what he would do. He was smart so I figured he would stay in the background, but now that he was known by the three army members who brought him in that night as a new recruit sneaking around, he might not be able to fly under the radar as much.

A small group of the army members took my attention as they started to spar and a small circle formed around them. They were doing hand to hand combat as the group around them cheered them on.

"Ugh, so barbaric when they fight each other," Ellis said as she breezed past me back into the castle. "Come on, Lexi. I can't stand to watch violence like that."

I joined her inside the castle and shut the window, already missing the warmer air and sunshine.

"Can you?" she asked me.

"Can I..." I answered, confused.

"Don't you hate violence?" she repeated.

"Oh... um, yeah, of course," I said. Memories flooded my brain of me patching up Cole's stab wound, treating Ally after the fire, fighting with Nate, Wren, even Damion when I first met him and realized that my ORC life was filled with violence. I wasn't proud of it, but it was my way of life right now. I wasn't above using violence if it was to protect the people that I loved.

"I know. Those army men. Ugh," Ellis said and pulled the curtain shut, blocking the sunlight out. A look passed across her face that I couldn't quite place, but I didn't want to ask her about it. She walked away from me and I did the only thing I could do next, which was to follow her.

The rest of the morning passed uneventfully with no more surprise royal visits. Ellis and I were in the staff quarters as she finished up her lunch while sketching me a map of the castle. I had asked her to draw the Lodge on the map for me too, telling her it was so I could avoid the area and not accidentally stumble upon it.

I was changing my clothes in my room since Ellis said my castle chores were done for the day and I could wear whatever I wanted now. I didn't have many choices so I settled for a white t-shirt with a pocket and a pair of fitted, stretch pants that went just above my ankles. There was no place for me to store a weapon so I kept it hidden in my bedroom under my mattress.

I fixed my hair and emerged back into our staff kitchen. I found Ellis sitting there with a t-shirt and shorts on, although her bun was still perfectly positioned on the top of her head. The way she was sitting with her legs crossed, I could see part of that scar peeking out from her shorts on her left leg.

I was a little bit inspired by her, her attitude, and the speech she had given me this morning about my scars. She had left a zip-up jacket for me to wear on my bed but I was working on embracing my scars and not covering them up.

She was still working on the map for me as another girl approached her. She leaned over the table and pointed to the map and said something to Ellis and the two of them giggled. Ellis looked up when she laughed and saw me and waved me over.

"Lexi, this is Brooke, she is a staff chef so she makes a lot of our meals and will often assist in the main kitchen," Ellis said, introducing me to the girl at her side.

"Welcome!" Brooke said and held out her hand. She had perfectly tanned skin, wavy brown hair, and was a few inches taller than me.

When I took her hand to shake it, her perfectly tan skin was also perfectly soft.

"I was just telling Ellis here that she should put the spots where you can get the best view of the army workouts on your map," Brooke said with a laugh.

Ellis rolled her eyes with a smile.

"Don't listen to her, Lexi. Brooke just likes to stare at them all day long, but we have better things to do," Ellis said, giving Brooke a light shove.

"Oh, I know the laundry and the folding won't do it-self!" Brooke said and jumped back in time as Ellis tried to swat her with my map.

"It's nice to meet you, Lexi. If you have any skills in the kitchen, I'd sure love to see them sometime. See you," Brooke said and turned to go. She headed back towards the double doors to the main kitchen to presumably start getting ready for dinner.

"All done!" Ellis announced and held the map out to me. "And I did put those spots Brooke mentioned on here."

I analyzed her map and realized it was on several pages of paper to indicate the several floors of the castle, which she so kindly labeled for me as well. She just unknowingly handed me the key to my and Cole's escape.

"Thanks for doing this," I said and tucked the map into the side pocket on my pants.

"I'm going to leave you on your own tomorrow, but you'll be doing linens upstairs so you should be fine," Ellis replied. She hopped off the kitchen stool and headed for the back door that she had led me through last night when she found me. She gave me a nod to follow her so I did.

The warm air hit me again as we exited the staff entrance and I forgot how happy it made me. I felt a smile spread across my face.

"Wow, that's a big grin," Ellis commented as she walked down the path.

"I like being outside, that's all," I answered with my smile still plastered on my face.

Ellis and I walked past the gardens and the barn structure that we saw earlier and she sat down under a cluster of skinny trees with low-hanging branches. I noticed that it was an apple tree and had a few apples on it, although they were smaller than I was used to seeing.

"Pull two off for us," Ellis said, gesturing with her hand.

I obliged and reached up to a high branch and pulled two apples off the tree with a tug before sitting down next to her and handing her one. I stared at the red fruit in my hand as it reminded me of my birthday with Cole. It also reminded me of a time before I joined the ORC, met my siblings, learned the truth, and life was simpler.

I felt my eyes start to fill with water and I tried to blink the tears away before they fell.

"What are you thinking about?" Ellis asked softly.

I sighed. I really needed to get my emotions in check.

"Someone I miss a lot," I answered as I took a bite of the apple. My face twisted at the slightly sour taste. That helped squash those tears right away.

"You want to talk about it?" she asked.

"Not really," I answered honestly. "How about you? You have some disdain towards the army."

Ellis turned to look at me, a slight look of surprise on her face. It shouldn't have been too much of a surprise with all the hints she dropped, expressing her dislike for the army since the moment I met her.

"They took someone that I miss a lot," she answered, using my own words.

"Took? As in recruited?" I asked.

She nodded quietly.

"He was my best friend and they recruited him and then he chose them over me," she said sadly. "He did his three years, all while I worked here so we could be close and then his three years were up... and he didn't leave. Said that he wanted to stay and that I didn't fit into his new lifestyle."

My heart hurt for her and I could see the pain on Ellis' face as she told me this story. It must have hurt to wait for three years and then not get the end result she wanted. I was surprised she opened up so much to me, someone she had just met a day ago but the heartache was probably too great.

"Was this recent?" I asked.

"About a month ago, his three years were up," she said.

"A month ago!" I found myself repeating rather loudly, shocked at how fresh this wound was. "I'm sorry, Ellis. That's really... terrible."

I wasn't sure what to say, honestly. I knew heartache from losing Cole and then being told he was the cause of the original fire from when I was a child. The emotional rollercoaster I had taken recently was wild and unpredictable, as were many things in my life right now, so I understood how upset Ellis probably was. I assumed she used her job and her excellent work ethic as a distraction.

"What was his name?" I finally asked her after a silence, deciding that if I ran into him when getting Cole out, I would give him a quick ass-kicking from her.

"Oliver," she answered, "but it doesn't matter now because he chose that life and I chose this life."

"Ellis, I'm sorry," I said and took her hand.

After a moment, she pulled her hand away from mine, not unexpectedly, and then stood up.

"I have to go help Brooke set up the dinner service. You enjoy this time outside and I'll come get you later," Ellis said quickly and left me sitting under the tree.

As she walked away, I could see her wiping her eyes with her arm and I sighed. I didn't mean to make her upset, but I knew her pain and I felt for her. I looked down at the apple I had pulled for her which she left on the ground.

I leaned my head back against the tree, let out a breath, and closed my eyes.

When I opened them again, the sun had moved its position and was beginning to set. I jumped to my feet, surprised at myself for my carelessness of falling asleep and cursing myself for not using the time to explore or analyze and memorize the map that Ellis had drawn me.

A loud cluster of sounds drew my attention to the barn, followed by someone yelling. Against my better judgment, I went towards the barn to see what the source of the sound was.

I crept to the side of the red-orange structure, around an old, dirt-covered pick-up truck that probably lived in that spot, to look in the side door instead of the two main doors that were open in the front. I poked my head through the side doorway and didn't immediately see anyone or hear anything so I decided to enter the barn.

I took a few steps in, looking up and scanning for anyone who might be hiding in the lofts above but there was no rustle of hay, no footsteps, nothing. I took one more step and kicked something over, spilling its contents across the barn floor.

I cursed myself and looked down and was surprised to see that it was a quiver and I had knocked it over and spilled all of the arrows on the ground. The bow that I assumed went with it was carelessly thrown on the ground next to the now empty quiver.

"Hello?" a voice called and I crouched to the ground. I wrapped my fingers around an arrow and my right hand around the bow and placed the arrow on the string. I slid my body behind a barrel and held my arrow taut.

I listened as footsteps crunched across the barn floor towards my direction. They were slow and unsure, and the person, a male I could tell from the deeper voice, was not trained like I was. I decided it was likely not a member of the army and poked my head out from behind my hiding place and got my first glimpse at the other person occupying this barn with me.

His back was to me, but he was tall, with a muscular build not quite as impressive as Cole's, and had a head of short dirty blonde hair like mine. He was looking up at the lofts, like I had been doing and taking slow steps backwards, unlike I had been doing. He was dressed in a white shirt and light blue shorts, similar to the color that Ellis and I wore today.

I stood up from my hiding spot, still holding the bow and arrow loosely pointed at the ground and decided this person was probably not a threat. If he turned around and was a threat, I could get this shot off faster than he could even think.

Finally, his uneven shuffled steps turned him around to face me. His face was handsome enough, he had dark brown eyes, was clean shaven, and had some serious cheekbones. My eyes traveled down to his hands which were clutched together in front of his waist and the bright red stain on his shirt.

"Hi there," he said to me. His eyes flicked to the bow and arrow in my hand and then back to my face. "You might hurt yourself there with that."

"Looks like you already did," I replied and nodded at him. The blood stain on his shirt was fresh and every few seconds, a drop of blood would slide out of his hand which was clenched in a fist. I watched them land on the ground and could see the small trail he was leaving while he walked.

"Actually, I cut my hand on a glass bottle over there," he said gesturing with his head to the other side of the barn. "I was trying... um, never mind."

I didn't say anything for a minute.

"Do you, um, have a name?" he asked after I didn't reply.

"In fact, I do," I said, smirking at my cleverness. "You first." I wasn't totally sold on this stranger yet.

"First, you put that down," he answered, pointing at the bow in my hand.

I decided that was a fair request and put the bow and arrow on the ground. I crossed my arms and looked at him trying to look tough and waited for him to speak again.

"My friends call me Fitz," he said.

"My friends call me Lexi," I answered.

"I would shake your hand but..." Fitz said and held up his bloody fist.

I crossed the space between us quickly and without thinking. It seemed to surprise him and he took a slight step back. I reached my hands out to look at his hand. He didn't stop me as I uncurled his fist and looked at the cut on the inside. It wasn't deep at all, but enough to make him bleed and the way he was curling and uncurling his hand wasn't helping.

"I was going to get that medical kit on the wall over there and see if there was something in there," Fitz said and threw his head towards the front of the barn where there indeed was a white box with a red cross sitting on a shelf there.

I grabbed the medical kit, opened it, and started digging through it. It had some antiseptic wipes, which I would need and then I just took some gauze cloth and tape out.

"This is going to sting," I said.

"Hey, I can take... OWWW!" Fitz started and then his tone changed when I wiped the cut with the antiseptic wipe. "Ow, ow, OUCH!"

"Hold still, you wimp," I said, keeping a firm hold on his hand as he tried to pull it out of my grasp. I placed gauze on the cut and then wrapped it around a few times before taping it so it stayed put. "Good as new."

"Seems like you've done this a time or two," Fitz said as he examined his newly bandaged hand.

"A time or two," I repeated and put his medical box back on the shelf. "Do you work here?"

The corners of his mouth turned up for a second.

"Basically," he answered. "I'm here every day, but I've never seen you out here before." He took a step towards me and stepped on the arrows I had left on the ground from when I kicked it over.

"Oh, sorry, I'll get those," I said quickly and picked them up and put them all in the quiver, and handed over the bow to him. He took it in his uninjured hand.

There was a brief silence between us.

"Well, I have to go," I said, breaking the quiet. "Keep the cut clean and covered, it should start to heal by tomorrow as long as you don't aggravate it and make it keep opening."

I turned and headed out the main barn doors heading into the sunset and back towards the castle. Although it was quiet, the gasp that escaped Fitz's mouth when he surely got a glimpse of my arms and my scars was not lost on me.

"Lexi, wait!" he called but I did not stop.

I continued out of the barn and headed back to the castle to see if anything needed to be done before the end of the day.

I wasn't sure who that young man that I just met was, but he wasn't built like Cole or I, always on the offensive and the defensive. I wondered what he had been doing in the barn anyway, I guess working as he said. I brushed the thoughts aside as I entered the staff entrance and back into my temporary home waiting for the cover of night to sneak over to the Lodge.

12

I woke up early, but before the sun to make sure that I still had the cover of darkness to sneak out. I decided that I would wait until the early morning hours so that if I ran into another person, I could say that I was out for a morning jog if they asked.

I dressed in all black, thankful that Ellie had given me a jacket the day before. I did bring my knife with me since I didn't know what or who I would find along the way so I tucked it into my ankle holster and secured it on my right side.

I glanced over the map one last time but I knew where I was going. Finding the Lodge was the easy part. Finding Cole inside the Lodge is where it would get dicey. I hadn't thought that far ahead in my plan yet, but I decided that I would figure that out in the moment.

I pulled on my backpack and looked around my room one last time. They were nice furnishings while they lasted, but it was more important for me to find Cole and get us out.

I crept out of my room and down the hallway. No one stirred and no one emerged from their rooms as I headed for the staff entrance. I twisted the doorknob and tasted the cool morning air as soon as I was outside. I took a deep breath and started to jog. It gave me the feeling of freedom like when I rode my bike for the first time with the wind flying past my face. I just hoped that I could get Cole and I to freedom once more.

I made it through the forest and over to the Lodge without any interruptions. I stood outside the largest structure and peered into the window. It was dark on the inside and I sensed no movement so I entered the main building. I decided I was looking for an office or anything that would possibly list where all of the different recruits were staying.

The main building was a spacious open room with long tables and benches for eating. The ceiling was vaulted and high and my eyes had already quickly adjusted to the darkness inside.

I went for the hallway at the end of the room but was disappointed to find only restrooms, the kitchen, and storage. I made my way back to the front of the large room and noticed a door towards the side that I didn't see before. To my surprise, a small plaque on the front of the door said "Office." The door was unlocked so I let myself in.

The room was small with one window that was half covered with a curtain. It had a square table in the middle with several mismatching chairs around the table and one wall that was covered with cabinets from floor to ceiling.

I immediately went for the cabinets and started rifling through them. I didn't dare turn the lights on for fear of attracting attention so I had to go slowly making sure my eyes fully adjusted as I read each of the folders that I removed from the cabinets.

Most of them discussed different training exercises, methods of recruitment and even some sort of army training manual. The front of the manual was stamped with "Middletown Army Property," making it the most official document I had seen all day. Everything else I had read so far was rather casual, mostly handwritten or typed but wrinkled. I rolled my eyes remembering that the Army was only men and that they were a mess.

Finally, I found a folder that I thought would help me labeled "Current Recruits." The label was not typed but written in pen. However, the list inside was typed and had a list of eighteen names on it, the last one being handwritten at number nineteen and it read *"Cole S."* I didn't know what the S stood for but I'm sure Cole didn't offer up his real last name with us being wanted fugitives in Odessa. Next to the names were numbers and next to Cole's name was the number two, which I hope corresponded to him being in the second dorm building.

I put all of the files away and left the office, pulling the door shut behind me. As I was about to leave the Lodge, I heard footsteps outside. The footsteps were deliberate and were getting louder, heading in my direction.

I ran for the door and stayed low as it swung open and I tucked myself behind it as a figure strode into the hall. They stopped a few paces in and before the door swung closed, I maneuvered my body through the opening in the door and back outside. I held my breath, deciding where to move next.

"Searching the Lodge now," I heard the man who entered say. "Is this where the motion was detected?"

I heard a radio crackle and then "Affirmative."

I ran on light feet putting as much distance between myself and the Lodge as possible. They had some sort of motion sensor that alerted them to my presence inside of the Lodge. I should've known there was some hidden security measure; it was much too easy to get in there.

As I ran back towards the castle, I decided that my mission wasn't a total failure. At least I knew that Cole was there and that he was likely in dorm number two. It had only been one day, I could try again tomorrow morning but I also decided that I needed more information before going in again and I should have been more prepared.

I jogged up the last hill away from the Lodge and the castle came into view. I let out a little laugh as I realized I wasn't leaving quite yet even though just an hour earlier, I thought I would be. The morning was quiet as I slowed my jog to a walk when I got near the barn. I faced the Lodge and I watched the sun start to come up over the building. I thought of every sunset that Cole and I ever watched together growing up and felt that stab of pain that I knew was longing for him.

I wandered around the side of the barn, not sure what to do with all of my extra time this morning. I peered inside and didn't see any signs of the bleeding man that I found here yesterday so I went inside.

The bow and arrow I had stepped on was hanging on the wall and the space had been tidied up. I could still see a few drops of blood on the ground and I followed them over to the wall where he said he had cut himself. Indeed there were bits of broken glass on the ground. I examined a shelf that was at my eye level that had various items on it like another glass bottle, various size metal cans, and even a few pieces of wood.

Based on the dents and the many holes in the wall, it looked like that man was trying to hit the items... but was missing much more than he was hitting.

"Looks like target practice," I wondered aloud and put my hand on the wall.

"Indeed," a voice said from behind me.

I spun quickly to a man dressed in all black and his hood up, with the bow in hand, an arrow pulled taut and pointed right at me. I put my hands up to show that I was not armed when I realized it was the man from yesterday.

"It's you," I said to him. "Fitz, right?"

"Don't move," he shouted to me from the doorway, shaking his head so his hood fell back.

I obeyed his command, not entirely in the mood to take an arrow to the chest today. Although I looked at his hands and even despite the distance, I could see him struggling to hold the arrow in place against the threading with his right hand. There were no guarantees which way that arrow would fly if he let go.

"Two times in two days I find you here," he called nervously. "Who sent you?"

"No one," I answered and took a slow but big step towards him. "I was exploring, just like yesterday when we met."

I took another step.

"Exploring this barn again? There's rarely anyone out here," Fitz said.

Another step.

"Seemed like a quiet place to come and think," I offered. Another step.

I was trying to get close enough to him to disarm him without getting shot. But I was also banking on his wobbly hold that he wouldn't hit me if he did let his arrow fly.

He was quiet so I took another step towards him, still with my hands up so he could see them.

Fitz took two steps towards me and now was only about two feet from me but still armed.

"I told you not to move! Did they send you?" he said.

"They?" I repeated. "Who's they?"

"The M.A. I know they have spies and they've been spying on me, reporting to my father about my skills. They should be happy I'm trying to improve off of their time,"

I watched his fingers fiddle with the string of the bow again and I made my move. With my hands already raised, I quickly reached out with my left hand and wrapped it around his wobbly arrow and pulled. The arrow came free instantly due to his poor grip and was now in my grasp. I took my right arm, which was bent at the elbow and clocked Fitz in the nose with it. He dropped the bow, clutched his nose and I scooped it up as I took a few steps back from him.

"Ouch, man!" he yelled through his hands covering his face.

I stood in my spot and he didn't come for me or take a swing at me, he just rubbed his face for a few minutes before he finally looked at me.

"Who the hell are you?" he asked.

After seeing him yesterday and today and his lack of combat skills, I made the risky choice to decide that he wasn't a threat to me.

"Lexi, from yesterday," I answered. "I'm... new staff in the castle. I work with Ellis."

I decided to show a gesture of good faith and I stuck out my hand to him since we didn't shake hands yesterday when we met. He hesitantly took it and then we shook hands.

"You're one of the maids?" Fitz asked me.

"I guess so," I replied with a little shrug. "I'm new in town and Ellis helped me out."

He eyed me and the bow in my hands. "Do you even know how to use that?"

I answered him with a nod of my head.

"Go ahead then," he continued and gestured towards the wall I had been examining before. He held out the quiver full of arrows to me.

"Best of three," he challenged.

He hadn't even finished those words before I pulled two additional arrows from his quiver and shot them with the one in my hand towards the targets across the barn. My three arrows hit the glass bottle and two of the metal cans and they all crashed to the floor after being pierced by the flying arrows.

"Your turn," I said with a smirk and handed him the bow, although he did not take it. The look of shock on his face said it all. "Look, Fitz. I'm just a maid, as you say. I'm not a spy or anything for the Army. I'm just me, and I've had... a challenging upbringing." I decided those words were best to use to explain my situation.

"You seem... trustworthy. The army has been putting a lot of pressure on me," Fitz said, "to be better and fit in more with them and their style."

"Are they trying to recruit you?" I asked.

A whistle sounded in the distance back in the direction that I had come from. Fitz and I both turned our heads in that direction before he swiveled back to look at me.

"I have to go. I'm sure I'll see you around, Lexi," Fitz said and ran out of the barn towards the Lodge and left me holding his bow.

I hadn't completely figured him out yet. It would surprise me a little bit if the M.A. was trying to recruit him for his skills. His bow work was sloppy and he had no sort of combat skills that I could tell. He looked like he could be old enough and maybe they were really desperate for more people since the list I had found had less than twenty names on it.

I returned the bow and the quiver to the spot on the barn wall and headed back to the castle as the sun emerged over the horizon.

The staff quarters were quiet as everyone was likely still asleep for the next few minutes before we all arose for our morning duties. I snuck back into my bedroom at the end of the hall, indifferent to return for now since my first attempt at escape with Cole failed this morning. I changed into my blue dress and shorts and tied the blue ribbon in my hair trying to make it look half decent after running through the woods and sneaking into the Lodge earlier.

I was relaxing and studying the map when a knock sounded at my door. I got up and opened it to find Ellis standing there with a nervous look on her face. I also realized she was still in her sleeping clothes and not yet dressed for the day.

"What's wrong?" I asked, seeing the look on her face.

"One of the Army leaders reported a break in at the Lodge earlier this morning. I just wanted to make sure you were okay," Ellis answered.

"A break-in?" I repeated, feeling some heat flood my cheeks.

"Yeah. Nothing was stolen but someone was definitely sneaking around through their files," Ellis said.

"Could it have been one of the recruits?" I asked.

"Probably not," she replied. "They would know how to not trip the alarms they have installed. I heard that they're doing a full search of the property today, just to let you know in case you run into any of them in the castle."

"Ooh," I heard Brooke's voice before I saw her appear behind Ellis. "Army recruits in the castle? Up close, how nice." She flashed a pretty smile at us and then walked away, laughing.

"Oh shush, Brooke!" Ellis snapped.

I remembered Ellis telling me about her friend who was in the M.A. and left her behind to join after his three years of service were up. She probably was not looking forward to having the chance of running into him in the castle.

I, however, was looking forward to the chance of possibly running into Cole. I had to be careful and strategic if and when that moment came. I had been careless this morning setting off those motion sensors that I hadn't even known were there.

"It'll be okay, Ellis," I said to my friend and put my hands on her shoulders. "Go get ready, we'll have something to eat, and then go get started."

I gave Ellis a little push in the direction of her room to get ready and left mine to join the other staff in the kitchen. Someone, presumably Brooke, had left us a big basket of muffins and slices of bread for breakfast so we sat around munching on the baked goods while discussing the news of the break-in.

"It was probably a recruit trying to get ahead and see what challenges were coming up," one of the staff named Thomas had said.

"I heard it could've been one of those escapees from the other kingdoms," another staff member offered.

"But there were two fugitives. Don't you think they'd be on the run together?" someone else asked.

The chatter continued until Ellis reemerged to break up the discussion. She seemed to hold a leadership role here even though she was not the oldest staff member here by any means.

"Alright everyone, let's get started. The Army is going to be trampling through the halls and we need to stay ahead of the mess that they'll be bringing in," Ellis commanded.

The group began to disperse as she doled out assignments for the day. I was assigned to the second floor to stock the linens and straighten up the bedrooms. She sent us off to work with an extra warning of caution but I wasn't afraid. It's not like I was in danger; I was the one who broke in.

The morning went by quietly and without any significant events. A few times I heard the boots of M.A. members stomping down the carpeted halls and I made every effort to duck into a room or a closet to avoid them. I always stole a glance out in case Cole was among them but he never was.

After I finished all of the rooms on the second floor, it was just after lunchtime so I headed back to the staff quarters to grab a bite to eat and see if I was needed anywhere else.

I found Ellis, Thomas, and another older staff member named Rita sitting in the kitchen area. Rita was probably closer to Remy's age, her hair graying slightly but still long and beautiful. I learned that she often worked directly with the Royal Family members, bringing them the things that they needed during the day.

"There you are!" Ellis said when she saw me enter.

"Sorry," I replied automatically. "I wanted to finish up everything before lunch. What's going on? Any new updates on the break-in?" I tried not to sound too eager when I asked. I was hoping I might get a head start on an escape if they were closing in on realizing that it was me sneaking around the Lodge this morning.

"Not yet. They think they have some clues but they probably won't find anything concrete," Thomas answered disappointed. "I was hoping they'd catch a criminal and then throw them in the dungeon. Wouldn't that be fun?"

"Do we have a dungeon?" I asked.

"Do we have a dungeon!" Thomas repeated. "This is a castle! Of course we do! I'll show you sometime! But I've got to get back, the Army guys were permitted to have lunch here in the castle today and the dining room is a disaster. Help would be appreciated if anyone is free."

I was sure the dungeon looked like what I imagined a dungeon to look like: cold, dark, gloomy, and probably in the basement. I never got to see the one back home but Cole told me a little about it so I got the picture.

"I'm finished with my tasks, so I can help you after I eat," I offered as I took a premade sandwich out of our communal refrigerator and took a big bite.

"Actually, you've been requested by Prince Joseph," Rita said to me.

"Wha--?" I said, mouth full of sandwich. "The prince? Who is he?"

"He's the prince," Ellis answered sarcastically.

"I didn't get specifics. I just brought the message." Rita replied. "He will expect you upstairs in his library after the lunch hour when he returns."

"I think I put it on your map," Ellis said to me. "You've probably walked past it five times already today."

"But why me?" I asked cautiously.

Rita put her hand on my shoulder.

"Prince Joseph is very nice. I've known him almost his whole life so don't be worried. He probably just wants to meet the new staff member. He's young and kind like that," she said reassuringly then turned to head back to her duties.

I looked at Ellis nervously.

"Perhaps it's because you did so well in front of the King. Surely he said something to his son," Ellis offered and patted my hand. "Seriously, don't fret. Come join Thomas and I in the main dining area when you're done, okay?"

"Okay," I replied with a nod and put my sandwich down. I was nervous for more reasons than I cared to admit in front of my new colleagues. The top two reasons were my identity as an Odessa royal, and my identity as a wanted fugitive had been discovered.

Neither option was great.

My nerves prevented me from finishing my lunch so I stowed it away for later, went to freshen myself up in my room and then prepared myself to meet the Prince.

As I left the staff quarters and wandered through the halls, I wondered what he would be like. I presumed big-headed, remembering the fireworks that were launched to celebrate his birthday, in addition to the big party that the entire town threw in his honor. It had been quite the spectacle.

Now that I was on the second floor, I tried to remember which door was which. I opened a few closets and bedrooms until I opened a door that led me to a room full of bookshelves, armchairs, and a big fireplace made of brick.

I was alone in the room and the Prince didn't seem to be there yet so I walked the perimeter of the room running my hand along the books that were on the shelves.

I scanned the titles, looking for anything that might be interesting. I pulled out a couple about the history of Middletown, the Royal Family, and one about the founding of the Middletown Army that I thought might be helpful if I could find the time to read it and learn a little bit about their organization.

I kept an eye on the door as I flopped into one of the armchairs with my feet over the side and began reading the book about the Middletown Army. I was trying to read quickly to see how much I could learn, but the beginning was slow and I was having trouble digesting the material.

Suddenly the library door swung open and I jumped to my feet to show some sort of respect for the Prince who shut the door and turned around to face me.

Fitz stood before me and I let out a sigh of relief.

"Geez Fitz, I thought you were someone else," I said and sat back down in the chair, reopening the book where I left off. "What are you doing here, anyway?" I asked when he stayed standing by the door.

"Meeting you here," Fitz answered and crossed the room towards me. "What are you reading?"

"Ha," I replied with a laugh. "Nothing really. I've been summoned by the Prince."

"Indeed you have," Fitz said.

I peered at him over the top of my book trying to figure out what this clumsy guy was up to when he bent forward and bowed low towards me, causing my eyebrows to raise in confusion.

"Prince Joseph Fitzpatrick Cartwright," he answered with a smile, "but my friends call me Fitz."

13

I didn't move as Fitz stood back up to his full height. I was still lying lazily in the armchair trying to digest what he just said as I continued to eye him over my book.

"Huh?" I asked, closing my book and swinging my legs over in front of me. "Hold on."

I grabbed the book about the Royal Family that I had pulled from the shelf and began thumbing through the first few pages reading the table of contents until I found what I was searching for. I frantically flipped through the pages and read about the Royal Family of Middletown and sure enough, I saw his picture and name on the page as the son of the King and the Queen. Although it looked like the photo was a few years old, it had all of the same features as the person in front of me.

"Well I'll be damned," I said out loud.

I slammed the book shut and leapt to my feet, hoping I didn't just earn myself a quicker opportunity to see the dungeon.

"Sir… Your Highness," I stammered, trying to find the right words. "I'm so sorry."

Fitz let out a roaring laugh and had to support himself with his hands on his legs as he doubled over.

"Wow, Lexi, that was the funniest thing I've seen all day," Fitz said as he wiped a tear from his eye. "Phew, I really got you there."

"I asked you the first time we ran into each other if you worked here and you said you did!" I stated.

"No, I said I spent a lot of time here, but I never said that I worked here," Fitz corrected me with a smile.

"Well, you have summoned me for a reason, I presume," I said, folding my hands in front of me and trying to sound a little more formal in front of this man.

"You don't need to act like that, Lexi," Fitz said to me. "I liked the way you were before you knew I held a title."

I could understand his feelings about that. I remember how much Brayden had disliked me during ORC training and then after he (and I) learned my true identity, he became a different person towards me. And I will admit, I like that new person much better.

Fitz seemed very casual and I decided I would try to be casual around him too, and hopefully if I stepped too far in the wrong direction, he would correct me.

"Follow me," he said and walked over to one of the bookshelves on the far wall. He reached up to one of the shelves closer to the top and pulled out a dark red colored book. Upon his removal of the book, there was a loud click and the shelf swung forward and I watched Fitz slip away through the opening it left.

I didn't follow him until his head reappeared around the shelf and he gave me a nod to go with him. I also tucked through the opening and the shelving unit clicked closed behind me.

The space we entered was large with soft flooring and what looked like padded walls surrounding us. There were two windows that let in the natural light from the sun and allowed me to see the contents of the room.

I knew immediately it was some sort of training or exercise room. It had weighted equipment in it, a large cylindrical bag hanging in one corner, and a wall that was full of weapons. Some I had seen before but some I had not and I had no idea how they worked.

"What are we doing here?" I asked the prince.

"I need your help," he answered as he stopped walking and turned around to face me. "My father built this room so that I could train and become an elite member of the M.A., now that I'm of age to be recruited. He expects me to try out and win one of the Rank Leader roles but I don't stand a chance against some of the other guys in the Army. They're older and more experienced than me."

"So, what can I do for you?" I asked, although I already thought that I knew the answer.

"I need you to train me so that I can earn one of the Rank Leader roles," Fitz replied.

"Me? Train you? How could a staff member like me help you?" I said, innocently. "I'm just a maid, after all."

He rolled his eyes and looked at me sideways. Then he unexpectedly lunged at me. Fitz moved quickly for a clumsy guy and I barely dodged him at the last second.

He landed on the ground without a lot of grace but jumped back up and charged me again, his hands swinging wildly.

I ducked one of his hands and grabbed the other with both of my own and spun, twisting his arm awkwardly. The motion brought him to one knee and I used that moment to plant a kick right in his lower back and he flew forward onto his stomach.

Fitz climbed back to his hands and knees and turned around towards me again before falling back and sitting on the ground.

"Yeah!" he shouted. "Teach me that!"

I had my hands protectively in front of me and dropped them to my sides realizing that he had been testing me.

"You have some sort of training. I'm not going to ask where it came from or where you came from but I am going to ask you to help me. You have the skill set that I was always expected to have," Fitz said from the ground. He slowly moved to his feet and kept his hands up, surely aware that I could put him right back on the ground again if I needed to.

"I'll take care of your work schedule. You'll train with me and whatever you need or want in return, you can have. Does that sound fair?" he asked.

"Whatever I want?" I asked.

"Within reason," Fitz said with a smile, "I can't make you the Queen so if you wanted that, sorry. But just about anything else, I can do."

I mulled it over. I could give him some tips and he could give me access to the things that I needed in order for Cole and I to get out. In fact, he could probably get me access to Cole too. That alone made my decision very easy.

"I'll do it," I said and reached out a hand to Fitz to pull him off of the ground.

He leapt to his feet, not needing my help and clapped his hands together.

"You will?! Thank you so much, Lexi! You won't regret it! Anything you want, you can have!"

"If we're going to train, and presumably in this room," I said waving my hand around at the space we were in and then at myself, "I am going to need some different clothes."

"Done!" Fitz said. "I'll get you a new wardrobe that you can keep in here to wear for training purposes."

"So tell me about the M.A. and what's required to become one of these Rank Leaders," I said.

Fitz launched into his tale, telling me how men were recruited at twenty-one years old and they served for three years, similar to what Ellis told me. He told me that they train nearly every day and they train hard with exercises in endurance, physical strength, combat, and some weapons training. It surprised me when he said that they use guns here, but that the objects that they shoot out of them are "stunners" and nothing lethal, which I was thankful for. He said they would sting and knock you right out if you were ever hit with one.

Fitz told me that in two weeks they would begin the tryouts for Rank Leaders and it seemed similar to our ORC training. The best became Rank Leaders, working directly with the King and the Army Officials devising strategy, tactics, and other programs to further the training of the recruits.

I couldn't hide my smile when Fitz told me that the Rank Leader skills assessments changed every year and this year, they would include a weapons demonstration. Fitz confessed that he was, in fact, practicing his archery the first time that I had found him.

He was going to need a lot of work if we only had two weeks. His assets seemed to be his speed, his strength, and his endless knowledge. His weapons skills seemed to be zilch and his combat skills were comparable to that as he had demonstrated when he tried to attack me earlier.

I held off asking any specific questions about the M.A. or its recruits knowing that Fitz was very eager to supply me with whatever information or supplies that I needed and it wouldn't be a problem. I wasn't sure whether I wanted to mention Cole yet, but I decided patience was a virtue and I would have to wait.

"I have a question," I interrupted. "The M.A. doesn't notice your absence in the afternoons?"

"Not really. We start training very early in the morning with endurance so by the time we get our eight hours in, it's already the early afternoon. We are permitted personal training time to prepare for the assessments so I will be spending mine with you," Fitz answered with a mock salute.

"Protect your midsection and protect your head," I said to Fitz.

"What?" he asked and turned his head quizzically.

I threw a fast punch right into his gut and heard all of the air leave his lungs. His hands flew to his abdomen and he took a knee. I was surprised he didn't end up completely on the floor and he was able to hold himself up after that hit.

"Protect your middle and your head," I repeated and put my hands in front of myself like I had earlier when he originally attacked me. "Keep your weight on the balls of your feet so you're able to move quickly."

I threw another punch and he slid to the side, dodging my hit. I spun quickly and went for his unprotected side and my closed fist made contact.

Another "oof" sound came out of the prince and I took a step back and smiled at him.

"Dammit," he said, holding his side but he didn't look discouraged as I came for him again.

He probably dodged a little more than half of my attempts and was only improving as time went on. He never once made a move to attack me so I figured it was best to just work on his defensive moves today before we jumped to offensive moves. His speed helped him a lot with keeping away from me even as I continuously came at him.

I had just lunged for him and he ducked low then rolled away from me. He came to his feet with his back to me and raised his arms triumphantly. I swung my foot out at him.

"Ha! You..." was all he got out before I swept his legs right out from under him and he landed flat on his back.

"Missed..." he finished with a groan as I stood over him.

"Don't turn your back on your opponent, Fitz," I instructed and I pulled him to his feet.

"Where did you come from?" he asked as he wiped the sweat off of his forehead with his arm.

"You wouldn't believe me if I told you," I answered honestly, knowing that my tale was... unique.

"But someone trained you in combat, weapons, and medicine," Fitz said to me. "You patched up my hand pretty good for someone who hasn't studied medicine, so I made an assumption there."

"A good friend did. He wanted to make sure I could handle myself if I was left alone," I answered, trying to keep my answers simple.

"Well, he did a pretty good job. We could use someone like him in the M.A. here," Fitz replied.

"I think that's enough for today," I said, changing the subject. "We can meet here again tomorrow, and we'll do offensive moves and review the defensive moves. Okay?"

"And I'll have a new wardrobe brought here for you," Fitz said and stuck out his hand at me.

I took his hand and he shook mine again before heading for the secret door and nodding at me to follow him.

"You know the way out?" he asked.

"I do," I answered heading for the door. I threw a look back at the books that I wanted to read but didn't know if I could take them out of here.

"You have full access to this room at any time if you want to come back and finish your books," Fitz said. He had been watching my internal struggle.

"Thank you," I replied. I gave him a nod and left the library.

I wiped my forehead with my arm and tried to flatten out my dress now that it was full of wrinkles. I pressed on my hair to squash any of the lone pieces sticking up after rolling on the floor all afternoon. It had to have been a few hours but I still headed for the dining room where Ellis and Thomas had told me they would be.

When I arrived there, the room was empty. The long table had been cleared and only placemats were on the table, indicating that there would be no dinner served in here tonight.

I decided to head back to our quarters, change out of my wrinkled dress and spend the remainder of the day outside. I was going to try to get a glimpse of some of the M.A. members and their training to see how much work Fitz really needed.

Again, there was no one around so I changed quickly and headed for the grounds, enjoying the sun as I walked outside. I went past the barn and along the outskirts of the trees that shielded the Lodge from my view. I knew it was there but I was trying to keep some space since it was just this morning that I had broken in.

I continued to move parallel to the Lodge and their dormitories, following faint voices and the unmistakable sound of a bowstring being released and arrows soaring. I stayed within the trees and leaned out to see what was occurring in the open field just ahead of me.

There were several guys all dressed in the same sort of dark navy blue camouflage that I was getting used to seeing standing on one end of the field and firing arrows at various targets at the other end of the field where several more guys were standing. They were off to the side of the targets; I just hoped for their sake that no one was that terrible of a shot.

I heard a stick snap from behind me and I spun around. The space was empty but I hung close to the tree and stepped behind it, hiding myself from view. Just as I had tucked myself away, I heard more rustling and held my breath hoping that no one would spot me.

I wasn't sure what would happen if I was caught. Would they think I was a spy as Fitz had thought? I circled around the tree keeping the rustling and the footsteps on my opposite side until they stopped moving, so I stopped moving.

I stayed still for a while until I peered out from behind the tree and saw a figure spying on the M.A. members just as I had been, in the same spot where I had been standing minutes before. I leaned out a little more to see the short, feminine figure with a bun perfectly done up on top of her head and a very recognizable light blue ribbon still in it.

"Ellis!" I whispered, causing the girl to shriek and nearly jump out of her skin. She whipped around to face me.

"Holy stars, Lexi. You scared me to death," she answered, clutching her chest. "What are you doing out here?"

"Watching them train," I replied. It wasn't a lie. "What are you doing out here?" I asked her.

"Um, me too," Ellis answered hesitantly.

I stepped out from behind the tree and put my hands on my hips and looked at her. I could tell she was lying by her nervous movements.

"Ugh, okay, fine!" Ellis said and crossed her arms. "I just wanted to see if I could spot Oliver. There, I said it. Okay?"

I wanted to tell Ellis that even though I was trying to gauge the M.A. members' training levels, I was always secretly looking for Cole and I could understand the hurt and the longing she was feeling.

"Do you come out here a lot?" I asked her.

She shook her head.

"Not really. I'm usually too afraid to come here. I don't want any of them to see me. The M.A. can be jerks sometimes," Ellis answered.

I joined her at the edge of the tree line although we stayed back enough to not be spotted. Tall grass stood outside of the tree line so we were hidden well enough behind it.

"Which one is he?" I asked as I watched several of the guys fire their arrows and bury them in the targets. None were direct bullseyes, but at least they were within the two-foot wide round target. I filed that note away for later.

"I don't see him," Ellis replied, pushing aside some branches and taking a step closer.

"Ellis," I said cautiously, but also too late.

She stepped on uneven ground and tripped forward and the upper half of her body tumbled out of the trees, flattening the grass and I watched every person's head turn in our direction.

I grabbed her midsection and yanked her back, hoping that the M.A. would leave that little disturbance alone but boy, was I wrong.

Every member that was in that field came running right towards us as I pulled Ellis to her feet.

"Run!" I told her and pushed her towards the way we came.

"I'll never outrun them! You go and leave me behind," she said, looking frantically behind me.

I looked around quickly, realizing the trees in our immediate vicinity were much too wide to climb and the branches were too high for either one of us to reach on our own. Although, I could boost Ellis up there and try to outrun them. I decided that was the best plan.

"Ellis, I'm going to boost you up there and you're going to climb into those branches and not move, okay?" I said.

"What? That's crazy. What about you?" she asked.

"I'll be okay. We have to do this right now or we are both caught," I said. "Ready?"

Ellis nodded at me and I interlaced my fingers together and bent my knees. She understood her role and took a few steps and then stepped into my hands and I launched her upward so she could grab one of the branches. She did so beautifully and scrambled her way into the tree.

"I'll come back for you!" I said and I took off running back towards the castle.

I hadn't even put twenty feet between Ellis and I before I heard the sound of footsteps breaking through the trees. I leapt over tree roots, fallen branches and tried to weave my way between the trees to lose them but they were hot on my trail.

I took a quick and sharp turn and pulled myself into one of the trees and hung on the branch as the literal army of men ran underneath me until they were out of sight. I let out a sigh of relief and waited another minute before dropping down and turning to head back to Ellis.

I froze after I turned.

At least ten M.A. members stood before me.

"Cute trick," the one in the middle said. He had a bow in his hand but didn't have it pointed at me, although four others did have arrows drawn, pointed right at me.

Great.

I stood my ground but felt my stomach turn to knots as I was horribly outnumbered and I couldn't outrun flying arrows. Even though their aim wasn't perfect (that much I could tell from their target practice), it was true enough that at least one of them would hit me.

"What are you doing out here?" the same guy asked.

"I was taking a walk," I answered.

"You ran like you had something to hide," he said.

"I'm new around here and I didn't hear great things about you," I replied. "And I didn't want to stick around to find out. Come to think of it, I don't really want to stick around now." I turned away from them and heard two arrows whiz past both sides of my head and looked up to see them buried in the trees ahead of me.

"Why don't you come with us?" the guy said with a smile that didn't look friendly. "We don't take lightly to intruders."

I rolled my eyes and stayed rooted to my spot.

"Vic, just grab her," the guy said.

One of the guys with jet black hair that was pressed back with hair gel stepped out of the line and approached me. He was big, taller than Cole and I could see his muscles through his tight shirt.

"We can do this the easy way or the hard way," Vic said to me.

"I'm game for the hard way," I said and squared off with Vic.

In a second, eight of the guys had surrounded me and formed a close circle. There was no space for me to squeeze out or go anywhere.

"Still game for the hard way?" Vic asked me.

I sighed and dropped my fighting stance, standing up straight. I put my hands up in a mock surrender and then crossed my arms trying to look annoyed.

Vic came in close and grabbed my arm, leading me away from the circle of men and back towards the way I had come running from. His grip was tight but not terrible, so I didn't fight it. I didn't want to get clocked in the side of the head or anything.

We went back through the trees towards the open field and I looked up to Ellis' hiding spot with my eyes and shook my head slightly telling her silently to keep hidden.

"What's your name?" Vic asked as we passed under Ellis' tree.

"Lexi," I answered. "I work in the castle."

"You work with Ellis?" the first guy asked.

"Aw come on, Oliver, you have to get over her, man," someone else said to him.

"Yeah, she's in the past!" another one called.

I looked at the one who asked me the question and sized him up. He had short light orange hair that was very closely shaven to his head and a lot of freckles, which was a common trait I noticed amongst those with red hair.

"Ohhhhh," I said, drawing out the word and looking sideways at him. "So you're Oliver. I've heard loads about you. I heard that you..."

"Stop," the red head stated. Short and sweet.

Oliver took a step in front of me and stopped our forward progress just before we broke free of the tree line. His eyes never wavered from mine as he spoke to the other men surrounding us.

"Leave us," he commanded them. His eyes flicked away from mine presumably to Vic who was still gripping my arm rather tightly. After a few seconds, the grip slacked on my arm and I felt him let go of me as he walked past me and left the space. The rest of the guys followed him leaving Oliver and I alone.

"What has Ellis told you?" Oliver asked as soon as we were alone.

I took a step back to give myself some space from him in case he tried anything and massaged my arm.

"Not much actually," I answered, "sorry about the false pretenses in front of the boys." I shrugged my shoulders. "I heard you were together and you chose the M.A. over her."

"I had a duty to serve," Oliver replied.

"And you did your time, but you didn't leave the M.A. So you left her," I said.

"They let you think you can walk away," he said quietly, "but you can't. Especially not me."

I didn't say anything but crossed my arms waiting for him to go on.

"I climbed the ranks early on, excelled in combat, and became a Rank Leader, and the King himself requested I stay in the M.A. He told me to forget about my life, forget about her and he would give me a new life. I was set to go into the reserves and then the King summoned me," Oliver explained. He tipped his head back and ran his hands through his hair. I held my breath thinking he might look directly up at Ellis and see her.

"And that was that. He convinced you to stay and leave her," I said.

Oliver nodded at me. "My duty is to the kingdom."

I crossed the space between us in two strides and punched him right in the nose.

"How dare you do that to such a kind person!" I said and backed up again. I shook my hand out, the anger I had towards him let me hit him in poor form, hurting my own hand.

Oliver's hands flew up and grabbed his face as the blood poured through his hands out of his nose. I watched as he shook his hands too, letting the blood drops fall to the ground as he glared at me with malice.

"I'm not above hitting a girl," he said as he came towards me slowly.

"I've never heard that one before," I said sarcastically and put my hands up to defend myself, realizing that my emotions had prompted me to poke this very dangerous bear and now I had to be ready to pay the price.

Oliver moved a second later and launched himself at me. I pushed him aside but he came right back at me. He sent his fists towards me in a frenzy but I blocked all of his shots with my forearms and by ducking around them.

"Wow, you can actually fight... for a girl," he commented as our feet moved together as we went in a circle in the small space we were in.

I lost my footing over an unruly root and Oliver landed a solid hit to my sternum and I flew backwards into the tree that was concealing my friend. My hair fell into my face and I brushed it back just in time to see his fist hurling towards me.

I ducked and spun behind him, wrapping my arms around his neck and pressing in just as I had done to Wren the first day I met him and my brother.

Oliver took a few steps backward and slammed me into the tree trying to get me to budge but I held firm. It would only be a few more seconds before he passed out.

"Stop, stop!" Ellis' voice called from above me.

I immediately loosened my grip on Oliver at the sound of her voice and the sight of her jumping down into the space in front of us. I heard Oliver gasp in surprise and also at the opportunity to pull air into his lungs without my arms there as I released him completely.

He took a few steps towards her and she jumped back, her eyes fearful.

I delivered a kick to the back of his knees and he crumbled to the ground where he was much less of a threat to my friend. I circled in front of him and stood in front of her protectively, but he made no attempt to attack. He simply got to his knees and looked at her.

She had one hand placed on my back as she looked around me at him on the ground and I could feel her shaking.

"If this is the man you've become," Ellis started and I could hear her struggling not to cry. "Then thank goodness you left, you monster." Her hand removed itself from my back and she ran back towards the castle.

Oliver did not try to get up or follow her. He was still sucking in lungfuls of air after my attack on him. I decided he wasn't a threat to either one of us right now, and left him on the ground to chase after my friend.

14

I still hadn't seen Ellis by the following afternoon when I headed to my next training session with Fitz. He had come through on his end of the bargain and presented me with an entire wardrobe of much more practical clothes than the uniform dresses I had to wear. In just these two days, Fitz had done a really excellent job keeping up with me and the combat skills I had been showing him.

"Oliver said he tripped yesterday while walking, but honestly I think one of the guys probably punched him or something. They tend to roughhouse a lot," Fitz said. "Unless you did it!" He cackled laughing.

My hand had bruised from where I punched Oliver the previous dayand Fitz had noticed it and had been bugging me about it all afternoon.

"I guess I can ask him tonight when he comes for dinner," Fitz said as we were cleaning up the training room.

"Dinner?" I asked.

"Father is having some of the potential Rank Leaders tonight for dinner and discussions about who will be selected next," Fitz replied. "Didn't Ellis tell you? She'll likely be there to... uh, help, you know."

Fitz always got awkward when discussing the tasks of the staff. He said that the different statuses made him uncomfortable; he was expected to be one thing and I, as staff, was expected to be something else. He also told me I was the first staff friend he had ever had and he appreciated that I didn't freak out about his royal status.

When he told me that, it gave me a good laugh. If he only knew who I was...

"Could I take Ellis' place tonight?" I asked. "She has been... um, feeling sick today." I couldn't imagine her having to work and serve dinner to Oliver after everything so I was more than happy to try to help my friend and take her place.

"That's really nice of you," Fitz said. "Whatever works, she'd be up late anyway so it's probably best that she rests."

"Great, I will let her know," I answered and turned to go. "Also, Fitz?" He stopped what he was doing and flicked his head up at me.

"You really are doing a great job. You care about other people too. For what it's worth, which isn't much coming from a lowly staff member," I said smiling, "you have my vote."

He smiled back at me as I slipped out the door into the library and headed back to the staff quarters to find Ellis.

I found her sitting on an armchair in our quarters with her feet hanging off one end and her head hanging off the other end with her eyes closed.

"Ellis?" I asked as I approached.

On her upside down head, her eyes opened at me as she sat up.

"New outfit?" she said like a question.

I looked down confused and realized I hadn't changed out of the training clothes before I left Fitz like I was supposed to.

"Uh, yeah. Thanks," I said and sat down on the chair next to her and put my feet up on the table. They were sore from all the working and training.

"New shoes too?" she asked, eyeing my shoes, which were also new and definitely not what we wore while working in the castle.

We were both quiet for a while and I decided to go first.

"You okay after yesterday?" I asked her.

"Am I okay?" she repeated and spun to face me. "Are you okay? He punched you right in the chest!"

"I did hit him first," I said with a slight shrug. "Which I am sorry about."

"I'm not!" Ellis yelled and crossed her arms in a huff.

We were quiet again until she uncrossed her arms and looked at me.

"Are we going to talk about the fact that you have these insane karate fighting moves, punched and fought Oliver and were fully prepared to take on half of the M.A. alone yesterday?" she asked quickly and all in one breath.

I looked up at her.

"Would you like to talk about it?" I asked her. I had a feeling she was going to ask me about it after watching our little dance yesterday.

"Um, kind of! I didn't know you were a badass!" she exclaimed.

"I was raised... to protect myself in case those I relied on weren't able to," I answered. "And before you ask, I was not going to kill Oliver, I was just going to cut off the oxygen to his brain until he passed out."

I watched Ellis' jaw hit the floor, realizing that I probably could have left that last part out.

"You have to teach me how to do that!" she said and threw herself on the floor in front of me. "What if he attacks me?"

"Ellis, I don't think Oliver would hurt you. Me, maybe. But, he just needs to prove himself in front of those... meatheads," I said using her words from the first day we met. She smiled at my use of it too and shook her head.

"I think it would be helpful; I wouldn't be so afraid to go over there. I'm even afraid that a few of them are coming here tonight for dinner. Speaking of which, I have to go and prepare," Ellis replied and stood up.

"Actually, I took your spot for dinner tonight," I answered and stood up to match her height. "I heard that Oliver was going to be there so I volunteered to do it instead."

The small girl in front of me threw her arms around me and hugged me.

"A badass fighter, a nice friend, next you're going to tell me that you're the ninja who broke into the Lodge!" Ellis said while hugging me and I tensed.

"Let's keep my skill set between us," I said, hugging my friend back. I did not need Ellis figuring out that her joke was completely accurate.

We broke apart from our hug as Ellis spoke.

"I'll help you get prepared for tonight. It's not hard, really. You just serve the food, keep pouring the wine and don't drink it because it makes your head spin. You will be fine!" she said.

I remembered my first experience with too much wine which nearly got Ally and I killed while Nate set fire to our small cabin.

I briefly thought of my sister and where she was. I hoped, wherever it was, that she was safe, with Damion, and nowhere near Nate. It had been a while since I thought of my siblings and friends. I had been so swept up with getting to Cole and escaping, I had forgotten that they were all traveling as a group and trying to find me. Surely, they were heading in this direction - they might even catch up to us.

Then I remembered that I had been out for a few days after Nate stabbed me, that we had traveled in the woods for a while and that now we had spent a few days here in this kingdom as well.

As soon as I found Cole and we got out, I would tell him that we had to add my siblings and my friends to the list of people to find and protect.

After we found Remy.

I felt my breathing start to pick up as I got lost in my thoughts about how many people I loved were missing and I didn't know where they were. I was starting to panic and lose control.

"Lexi, it's okay," Ellis said, taking my hands and pulling me out of my thoughts. "I'll help you through this tonight! You're white as a ghost, so just sit down and I'll explain to you what you need to do."

All I could do was nod, push thoughts of my loved ones out of my head for now, and listen to Ellis as she told me how I was going to survive this experience.

—

I had survived being stabbed, shot with high velocity paint rounds at point blank range, two fires meant to kill me and yet, I was terrified of this dinner service.

I could cut off a man's oxygen supply, twist their arm out of the socket, and had the knowledge to inflict fatal injuries and yet, I was afraid to simply enter this room of royalty.

I stood outside the double doors to the dining room with a bottle of wine in each hand, and shaking. I recognized the King's strong voice through the door as he was likely the closest to the door and seated at the head of the table. I was very nervous to see Oliver and realized that in protecting my friend, I may have set myself up for failure if Oliver called me out on my combat skills.

I took a quick drink from the red bottle in my hand to steel my nerves. I looked at the bottles of wine in my hands and realized now the liquid levels in them were uneven so I took a sip from the white bottle to make them match.

I wiped the top of each bottle with my thumbs, as I caught the sweet aftertaste of the white wine. It was fruity and I remembered the night that Nate had so kindly helped me drink plenty of it to incapacitate me. Never would I underestimate him or anyone else again.

I took another breath outside of the dining room doors.

My task was simple. I had already done the meticulous part of setting the table and lining everything up perfectly before the guests arrived. Ellis had told me that now I was to go inside, they would choose if they wanted red or white wine, I would pour it and move on.

She was waiting just inside the kitchen area to guide me through this event. She had pressed my blue dress for me and helped me get my hair in a high bun like she did and tied the ribbon for me. The bun was actually nice and she even added a little braid in it because she knew I always wore my hair in a braid.

With her in my corner, I would make it through this task and this event.

I pushed open the door quietly and the conversation grew in volume as I entered the room. I let the door swing closed behind me and stood in my place for a moment as I took in the room. Two M.A. members had their backs to me on one of the long sides of the table, Fitz was at the head on the left and the King was at the head on the right. Directly across from me sat Oliver and Vic from yesterday and neither one of them looked pleased to see me.

I moved my eyes over to Fitz and he gave me a subtle smile and nod to reassure me. I moved over towards the King as I had been instructed to serve him first.

"Ah, darling, hello!" he boomed as I stood next to him. He held out his glass towards my red bottle and I poured it for him. "Wow, a heavy pour you have, dear! I guess it's a good thing Miss Ellis was feeling under the weather and you jumped in for her!" He let out a roaring laugh and the gentlemen at the table laughed too.

They were all dressed similarly in white button down shirts and dark jackets over them with matching pants from what I could see. They varied in color from black to navy to dark green.

I caught Oliver's eye as the King said that I was covering for Ellis, and surely he knew it was because of his presence. He glared at me and I swallowed the lump in my throat and just willed myself to get through the rest of this evening.

I moved over to Fitz to serve him next as Ellis had told me.

"I'll have the white wine," he said to me. I leaned over and poured it in his glass. While my body was covering the King's view he whispered to me, "You're doing a great job."

I smiled at him and the reassurance that he gave me and was happy that he was on my side. I was looking forward to tomorrow when surely he would tell me how this evening went from his point of view.

I turned to the gentleman to the right of Fitz and held out both bottles to him as the conversation continued around the room. I looked at the King in his perfectly pressed jacket and shirt which had black buttons that stood out against the white cotton.

I looked at the man that I was serving wine to, realizing that he had not yet made a choice and I was likely going to have to help him out.

But my breath caught, my heart stopped, and I felt like time stood still as I looked down at his beautiful green and steel gray eyes, which stared back up at mine.

I couldn't move. I couldn't breathe.

Ellis did not prepare me for this.

Cole cleared his throat before he spoke. "Which do you like?" he asked me. The words came out a little scratchy like he was also struggling to keep it together.

"I, um…" I faltered and I couldn't think of anything to say. My brain had melted upon seeing Cole and I was having a tough time speaking. I closed my eyes for a second and when I opened them, he was still there, smiling up at me and waiting for me to respond to his question, which he already knew my answer to.

"The white is very good, sir," I said with a smile. My use of the word "sir" caused Cole's smile to get even wider.

"Then I will take that one," Cole answered and held out his wine glass to me.

I filled it up generously as I had the other two before me. I watched his eyes run up and down my outfit as Cole had probably not seen me in a dress since the day he pulled me out of that fire.

I felt like I couldn't stop smiling as I moved around the room and filled the remaining guest's glasses. The only person I didn't know was the man next to Cole that they called Greg. But I recognized his face as one of the M.A. members from my altercation yesterday and he probably recognized my face too.

I poured Oliver's wine last and emptied the last of the bottle of white into his glass.

"Looks like your hand is a little bruised there," he whispered to me, grabbing it and squeezing it as I poured his wine. It caused me to wince a little at the pain but it was nothing I couldn't handle.

"Same could be said for your nose," I whispered to him. "Sir." I smirked as I leaned back from him and stepped away from the table.

I caught Cole staring at me and watched his eyes move from the bruise on my hand to Oliver's nose and he raised his eyebrows at me. I smiled at him and gave him a slight nod, causing a smile to spread across his face too. He used the cloth napkin from his lap to cover his smile as he realized that I was responsible for the bruise to Oliver's nose, and likely his pride too.

I slipped out through the doors and as they closed behind me, the tears fell. I knew that they were happy tears that Cole was here and alive and so close to me. I headed down the hall, wiping my eyes on the back of my hand just as Ellis emerged from the kitchen.

"Oh gosh," she said, looking at tears. "Was it that bad?"

I laughed a little and shook my head. "It was fine, I promise," I answered. I fanned my eyes and wiped the last few tears from them. "Just a... coughing fit. I'm fine."

"What's it like in there?" she asked. "Is Oliver behaving himself?"

"Mostly trying to get under my skin, but don't worry because I can give it right back," I answered.

"How's the new guy?" Ellis asked.

"The new guy?" I repeated.

"I don't know who he is," she answered, "just that they were talking about him when they went in. They said that he's a really new recruit but is really good and might be the first newbie to ever make rank leader. But I think his competition is Prince Joseph so they'll probably select him."

I didn't even think about what Cole's presence in the room meant. It meant that he was being considered for one of those leadership positions that Fitz was going for. Cole would beat him in a second for the position unless they took multiple people.

Then I wondered why Cole would have even said yes to the dinner and to becoming a rank leader if he and I have plans to escape and leave Middletown. I was trying not to worry too much about it. I'm sure he was just playing the part just as much as I was until we could figure out a way to get out.

I hadn't even realized that Ellis had replaced my depleted wine bottles with new ones.

"Hurry back! Brooke will bring in the first course soon," Ellis said and gave me a little push back down the hall towards the dining room.

I slid back into the room and positioned myself on the side of the room next to the door so that Cole had his back to me.

"Well, what other defenses do we have in place?" Cole was asking as I re-entered the room.

"The motion detectors were triggered so there had to have been someone inside the Lodge," Oliver answered. "I was on site within two minutes."

"I wanted to know *your* thoughts, Cole," King Joseph said and glared at Oliver before turning his attention to Cole.

"Well sir, I would investigate what the cause of the intrusion was. What was the person looking for?" Cole asked but then continued. "Might be able to narrow down who the culprit was if you can figure out what their target was."

"Thinking in the mind of the culprit," King Joseph said, putting his fingers on his chin. "Genius!"

"Nothing was missing. The only slight clue was that one of the filing cabinets wasn't closed all the way," Vic offered.

I felt my cheeks flood with color as they discussed the break-in that I was responsible for. Cole, nor any of the other men in the room had any idea that it was me. It would probably baffle them that it was a girl, and that it was me. But now that I was standing in the same room as Cole, I wouldn't have to go snooping around the Lodge after hours anyway. Hopefully he and I would get a moment to talk, but I didn't know when we would get that opportunity.

"Lexi, dear, are you alright?" The King asked, pulling me from my thoughts.

"Oh. Um, yes sir, my apologies," I fumbled.

"Did the news of the break in frighten you? Come, come over here," he said and waved me over with my two bottles of wine.

I went to pour him another glass but he put his hand out to stop me and placed his hand gently on my arm.

"I do not want my staff to be fearful while they live under my roof and I want to assure you that these gentlemen here, in addition to the entire army, will be doing everything to keep you all safe," King Joseph explained.

"Thank you, sir. I appreciate that," I answered quietly and I met his eyes. They were sincere and matched his words. It was nice that he cared so much for his staff.

I took a few steps back from him after he released my arm and returned to my task of filing the wine glasses. Salads were served, followed by extravagant entrees that filled the room with a delicious aroma. Brooke had surely outdone herself for this group of individuals.

My role for the remainder of the evening had been simple. I was clearing plates, refilling glasses and ensuring that everyone had what they needed. I kept myself behind Cole so as to not distract him, but earned myself many looks from Oliver. I assumed he and I would never quite stand on the same side.

At the end of the evening, King Joseph rose from his seat prompting all of the other attendees to jump to their feet out of respect. Fitz was the only one who did it calmly, as he had likely been used to doing that his entire life.

"Gentlemen, thank you for coming this evening. I hope you enjoyed yourselves and I wish you all luck in the up-coming Rank Leaders competition," King Joseph said. He shook hands with each of them and then stopped next to me as I opened the door for him. "If you ever need anything, please let me or my son know." He placed a hand briefly on my shoulder and then strode from the room and I let the door close.

I felt all of the men breathe out a sigh and drop their shoulders, now that the royal presence had left the room. A few of them undid their top shirt buttons and their postures changed drastically. They were talking amongst themselves casually and finishing up their wine when Fitz came over to me.

"You did great," he said quietly to me. "I'm sure Ellis appreciated you doing this."

"Thanks. How was the food?" I said, trying to be polite and not look overly friendly in front of the others.

"Excellent. Please tell Brooke she outdid herself... again," Fitz answered then he leaned in next to me. "These guys are my competition so we need to work extra hard in the coming days. That new guy, Cole, really impresses my father."

I nodded at him and he gave me a slight wave as he exited the room. Oliver was quick behind him and said nothing to me as he went past. Vic and Greg mumbled a goodbye to me as they walked past and followed Fitz out of the room.

This left Cole and I in the room alone.

We both stood there for a moment, looking at each other until the door swung completely shut behind the men who had just exited and we heard it click back into place.

Cole and I ran together and wrapped our arms around each other. I rested my face on his shoulder and inhaled his scent while squeezing him. I felt his muscles pressed against me, his strong arms around me and it warmed my entire body.

He took a step back from me but held my hands in his.

"Look at this dress, Lexi Palmer," Cole said with a smile as he admired my dress. His eyes traveled up my arms. "You are beautiful," he added as he gave me a twirl and admired my scars. He continued to never judge me or stare like others used to.

I had kept my eyes down most of the evening, but I think I stayed mostly out of everyone's direct vision to not be stared at. I mostly approached the table and then receded, keeping my back to the walls. I assumed everyone else was too preoccupied with the conversation, the food, and impressing the King to notice.

Cole held my hands and traced his thumb over my bruised knuckles.

"Did you punch Oliver?" he asked me casually.

I smiled and shrugged my shoulders.

"He wasn't very kind to one of my friends," I answered.

"Making friends here already? Now tell me, do you work in the castle?" He asked using his fingers for air quotes around the word "work."

"I seized the opportunity I saw to be as close to you as possible in order to find out where they took you," I explained. "I followed you all the way here and then once I knew you were at the Lodge, I just had to bide my time until I could find you."

"How did you know I was there?" Cole asked.

"Funny story..." I said with a nervous laugh. "I'm the one that broke in and went through the recruiting files to find you."

Cole smacked a hand to his forehead at the revelation of my news. I was afraid he would be mad but then he smiled.

"Of course it was you, because we couldn't find a trace of anyone. Bet you didn't know that they had those motion sensors though. You're lucky to have not gotten caught," Cole said.

"Oliver was there. He did respond fast but I slipped out the door and ran. No one saw me though," I reassured him. "But let's talk about you, getting noticed by the King, wanting to compete for a Rank Leader position?"

"I didn't want to. I was also just biding my time until I could make a run for it and try to find you. I had to at least try to not get my ass kicked by everyone else during training," Cole explained. "They're rough on their recruits though, it makes the ORC look easy. These guys in this room are not people to mess with so be careful around Oliver. Although, I will say that Prince Joseph is improving immensely so he might prove to be a worthy opponent soon."

"Are you going to compete?" I asked him.

"I mean, I was hoping we would get out of here since this was meant to just be a place we traveled through to find Remy," Cole answered.

I thought back to what Cole just said about Fitz improving and I thought that he would definitely deserve the role over someone like Oliver. I wanted to be able to help him get to that point. I also probably should tell Cole that I was secretly training Fitz and I was the cause of his skill improvement.

"I was really worried about you," Cole suddenly said, stopping my thoughts.

"You haven't learned by now that I can take care of myself?" I asked with a smile and stepped closer to him.

"Except for that time you were unconscious and bleeding to death?" Cole reminded me before pulling me to him and kissing me.

His lips were as soft as I remember and he wrapped his arms protectively around my middle pulling me so close to him that there was no space between us. I moved my mouth with his and tasted a hint of the wine. We stayed locked together for a few moments and when we pulled apart, we were both breathless. He pressed his forehead to mine and held me there.

"Ahem," a quiet voice squeaked from the doorway.

My eyes flew open and I jumped away from Cole, although he used one hand to sweep myself behind him at the sound of the intruder.

I turned to see Ellis standing in the doorway.

"Ellis!" I exclaimed.

"What's going on here?" Ellis asked and crossed her arms. "I saw everyone file out except for you and the new guy so I wanted to make sure you were okay... but I guess you are."

"Ellis, I can explain," I said to my friend and stepped around Cole.

"You better," she said, clearly upset with me.

"This is Cole, the new recruit you spoke about. We are... together, hence my great interest in the M.A. after arriving here. I was worried about him and I hadn't seen him until right now," I explained. I decided to omit some parts of the truth like our past, where we were from, what our plan was, and who we both really were. "He is the one who taught me how to protect myself... and he is not a meathead."

She eyed us both although I watched her lip twitch when I said "meathead." She didn't say a word for what felt like a long time. When she spoke, her tone had completely changed.

"Lexi! Oh gosh, I'm sorry for interrupting this reunion!" Ellis said and she gave me a quick hug before turning to Cole. "Nice to meet you, even if you are M.A."

"Well, not quite yet," Cole answered and shook her hand.

"You're not like the others, I can tell," Ellis said to him and dropped his hand. "Lexi, I'll help you clean up."

Ellis burst into action, stacking plates and dishes together.

"Let me help her," I said to Cole. "Come and find me tomorrow, I should probably steer clear of the Lodge and its inhabitants who are not my biggest fans."

"I will," Cole answered and placed a kiss on my forehead. "I'll find you. Always."

He slipped out of the room and disappeared. I felt the coldness linger in my now empty hand. I watched the door until it clicked shut again and turned to find Ellis grinning at me from behind a stack of plates.

"Okay, girl. Spill!" she demanded.

15

A week or so had gone by since my long-awaited reunion with Cole. He and I continued to meet nightly in the barn where I first met Fitz and we sat up in the loft and spent time together talking and planning. I had convinced him to let us stay until after the competition after I confessed to him that I was training Fitz in secret.

We had two days left before the competition, whatever it may be and I hoped that Fitz would be prepared. Cole acted as an informant telling me about the other members who were in the competition, as well as providing updates on how Fitz was doing when with the other recruits. I was always pleased with all of his updates, as Fitz had been doing a great job keeping up with the other recruits. Cole did say that Fitz was not able to beat him in combat yet but he had come close a few times.

Cole and I had also decided that he was going to perform slightly below his average so that he didn't secure the position and to give Fitz a better chance.

Our time together was wonderful and I enjoyed every moment. It was free of threats and I was starting to feel like I didn't have to look over my shoulder constantly. We had considered staying here permanently if we weren't still looking for and worried about Remy. Not to mention my siblings and my friends who were on my original mission team.

Ellis was very understanding of me wanting to spend my time with Cole. I continued to give her bits of information to satisfy her curiosity about us, but I was careful not to reveal anything that was too dangerous.

Cole and I were sitting in the loft and watching the sun go down from through the window in the side of the barn.

"We used to do this every evening growing up. Do you miss that?" I asked him, with my head on his shoulder.

"I miss the normalcy, or at least the familiarity," he answered. "Even on days we weren't together, I'd watch the sunset knowing that you were watching it too."

"So cheesy," I said to myself and shook my head.

He planted a kiss on my head and I closed my eyes. I was so happy and finally felt relaxed and nothing could take the smile off my face in this moment.

"Lexi! Lexi!" someone's hushed voice was calling from below.

My eyes snapped open and the smile disappeared from my face. I recognized the voice though so I didn't panic, unlike Cole who went into defense mode, grabbing the bow I kept stored up here.

I gestured for Cole to back up and I leaned over the edge of the loft and looked down at the top of Fitz's head.

We had also agreed not to tell him or anyone other than Ellis about our relationship.

"Fitz! What are you doing!" I asked him.

"There you are! Ellis said you were down here, or up there, I guess," Fitz answered. "We have a problem."

My least favorite words to hear.

"What's going on?" I asked. I felt Cole's body relax behind me but he stayed out of sight.

"The specifics for the competition have been released," Fitz said.

"Tell me what that means. Remember, I'm new here," I replied.

"The competition has been moved to tomorrow morning, first of all," Fitz started.

That got my attention and I sat up and leaned over the ledge more before he continued. "It used to be just an individual skills demonstration but this year, the skill sets have been chosen. So it's half combat skills and half a weaponry skills demonstration."

That wasn't good. I didn't know how to use those guns that the M.A. guys had pulled on Cole and I our first day in town. Fitz could perform well enough in the combat section but unless he knew how to use those weapons, he wasn't going to do well enough to rank high.

"How are your skills with guns?" I asked him.

"Guns?" he repeated and looked at me sideways. "The weapons demo is to be done with a bow and arrow."

I felt a small smile creep onto my face at that revelation.

No guns? No problem.

"Can you help me prepare for tomorrow?" He asked.

I stole a look back at Cole. His bow and arrow skills were nothing to brag about but he could probably hit a target, unlike Fitz who had trouble just holding the damn thing. Cole gave me a nod and motioned with his hands for me to go.

I ducked back from the edge so Fitz couldn't see and planted a kiss on Cole's lips.

"I'm going to try to help him. You'll be okay, right?" I whispered to him.

"Yes, now go help him. I'll wait til you guys leave and then head back to the Lodge," Cole whispered back to me.

"Good luck tomorrow," I said and squeezed his hand as I crawled over to the ladder. "Use my bow to practice," I added, nodding at the one in his hands and then climbed down from the loft.

Fitz and I left the barn at my request to give Cole a chance to sneak away and went to a secluded area of the woods away from the Lodge where he and I could practice.

I gave him all of the basics which, unfortunately, were taught to me by Nate. I helped him steady his hands and take aim and showed him how to anchor his shots with his thumb on his lip or cheek.

We had been at it a few hours as we lost the light from the sun. Fitz had only managed to hit the tree as a target one or two times. His arrows were wobbly and his form needed a lot of work.

It was finally dark when Fitz took his bow and threw it at the ground.

"I'm not getting any better! There is no way I'll be able to hit even one of the targets tomorrow," he said, pacing in frustration.

"Fitz, listen, you'll do fine. You just..." I started but he cut me off.

"No! They are going to be moving targets too. I'll be an embarrassment. They should be taking you and not me. You're a way better fighter than I'll ever be," Fitz said and sat down in defeat.

"What if..." I hesitated. "What if I shot for you? Maybe I could be far enough away that they wouldn't recognize me."

Fitz sat up abruptly and pulled me down to his level so suddenly he almost ripped my arms off.

"Lexi! That's genius!" he yelled, shaking my shoulders. "Because I'm in the competition, they are done blind this year. We have to wear these helmets so that when my father watches, he doesn't know which one is me so that the results are fair. We could trade places!"

I listened to his words. There were so many opportunities for mistakes, or getting caught. It was a good plan, but I felt like it had a lot of holes in it.

Sensing my doubt, Fitz grabbed my hands.

"I know that you, Lexi, can do this no problem. And if you'll take my spot for me, I would be forever in your debt. My father will disown me if I don't perform well, I know it. This has been his plan my entire life," Fitz explained.

I sighed knowing what my answer was going to be. After all, I had convinced Cole to stay this long so that I could help Fitz and we would've stayed for nothing if I walked away now.

"Okay, Fitz. Don't think I won't come and cash in that favor one day," I said with a smile at him.

"I'll make it two favors. You'll be glad you've got a prince in your corner one day," he said and straightened his jacket jokingly.

"Oh yeah, a prince who can't use a bow," I answered playfully with an eye roll. "Just tell me how we're going to pull this off."

Fitz double checked around us to make sure we were alone and then leaned in close.

"Here's what we're going to do."

16

It was the morning of the competition that Cole and Fitz (and secretly me) would be competing in. Fitz didn't tell me until late that they were starting early, which cut my sleeping window from short to even shorter.

We went over the plan many times, even walking the grounds with a flashlight so he could show me exactly where I was to go. I would have been concerned that we might be spotted but it had been so late and completely dark. He was lucky I had my impeccable eyesight or I would never be able to find my assigned spots in the morning.

Ellis and I had been tasked with bringing towels, water and medical supplies to where the competition was taking place. We both had other daily tasks we still had to complete for the day, and I had to get them done before sneaking off to meet up with Fitz.

At an earlier than usual hour, she and I headed over with the requested supplies and dropped them off. We were just leaving as the boys arrived, followed by likely the entirety of the M.A. who were there to watch as spectators.

Cole was walking with Fitz and they both looked up at us and gave me a small smile, which Ellis and I returned before heading back to the castle for our tasks.

"You know," she said to me once we were far enough away, "You would probably be a better choice than any of them. But maybe not when it comes to the shooting stuff, that might be hard."

I smiled at her compliment and at the fact that she was blissfully unaware of my skill set or where I was going to disappear off to today.

"I was hoping to try to watch them later. You think we'll get done in time?" I asked her.

"Oh yeah. I want to watch too, so it's good we have light tasks today. Should be done before noon," she answered.

That was good because Fitz wanted me to be waiting on standby at noon in case his name was pulled first. We were hoping it wasn't, but we couldn't guarantee anything at this point.

Ellis and I returned to the castle, and most people were still sleeping, which was fine. I was on laundry duty today and she was helping in the kitchen, prepping for the big party tonight in the great room when they announced who would be selected for the new roles in the M.A. She had said that they didn't need an occasion to throw parties, but that King Joseph liked to have gatherings of friends and guests in the castle often.

"More work for us but more fun for them," she had said.

We parted ways and agreed to meet and go watch the competition together, although I knew that I was going to have to sneak away without her noticing. It was hard to keep all these secrets from Ellis, as she and I had become close, but I decided that the less she knew, the safer she would be in case anything went sideways. It reminded me of why Cole and Remy kept those secrets from me about my past to themselves all these years.

I ran the clothes through the laundry faster than I ever have and folded everything with speed and precision that I didn't know I was capable of. It was mostly tablecloths and linens, likely for the party tonight.

I finished my tasks quickly. It was just about an hour before noon, so I headed to my room to change out of my uniform. I pulled on some regular clothes, even though I would be changing into clothes that Fitz left for me in the woods, so I would match the other competitors.

I successfully snuck out of the staff quarters, made my way to the barn where my bow and full quiver of arrows were ready and headed to the woods where Fitz had left the clothes for me. We had agreed on the location the previous evening and after throwing several looks over my shoulder, I bent low to retrieve the uniform from the hollow of a tree that we chose last night.

I put on several layers, making my appearance larger in stature, as Fitz was significantly more muscular than me. He was supposed to hand off his helmet when he came through here to take his spot. Although I had been nervous all night and most of today, everything was working out and I was glad that Fitz had planned everything out.

He was smart, kind, resourceful, a good enough combatant, and also cared a lot about people. He would make a great leader. He had a lot of the same qualities that Cole had, which made Cole an excellent member of the ORC and now the M.A.

I headed to the tree line and climbed my way onto some thick branches with lots of leaves that obscured me from sight of anyone walking by and waited. I watched as some recruits placed round circular targets in the open area. The targets were large and I didn't think they would be too challenging to hit.

Across the field, recruits had gathered on the sidelines and were getting ready to watch the weapons event unfold. I was curious to know how the combat event went this morning. I was sure Cole did well and I hope that Fitz did well enough too.

I could make out a group of guys dressed similarly to me so I assumed they were the ones about to compete. As they were ushered into the trees, King Joseph made an appearance and settled in front of the M.A. members on the sideline. He was dressed casually again with light brown pants, and a collared shirt with the sleeves rolled up.

The air was warm and I was starting to sweat in my many layers of clothing. I repositioned myself on the branch just as I heard footsteps approaching. I moved my head and saw the flash of light orange hair and knew it was Oliver. I held my breath and he passed by me with not even a glance in my direction.

The next time I saw him, he emerged from the trees with his helmet on covering his face so that the King (and others) couldn't identify him. He scooped up a bow and quiver and stood with an arrow already placed on his bowstring and aimed at the six targets.

A whistle blew and Oliver began launching arrows across the field. He put one in each target and then I watched as the targets started to move. I realized that recruits were behind each target and were instructed to move around with the targets in hand. That was a task I would not want.

The targets were large, likely wooden and probably pretty heavy, which prevented them from running at full speed with them. That would have definitely added another challenge to this event.

Oliver put several more arrows in the targets while they were moving and of the fifteen arrows that he shot, I counted that he made them all except for two. It was pretty impressive, I would give him that. He must have practiced a lot, I decided.

He put his empty quiver and bow down and returned to the forest. I watched him take his helmet off and shake his sweaty head. He looked satisfied with his performance as he passed underneath my hiding place and disappeared.

A few moments passed as another figure came through the trees, who I recognized immediately.

"Cole!" I whispered.

I watched him freeze and look around before he looked up towards me although I was fairly certain he still couldn't see me. I maneuvered myself and dropped down from the tree. With all of my layers, it was ungraceful and I tipped over and landed on my hands and knees. I clambered to my feet and stood before him.

"What are you doing here?" he asked.

Then he took in my appearance.

"You're going to pretend to be him, aren't you?" Cole asked me and crossed his arms.

I nodded at him.

"There was no other way with the short amount of time we had," I explained to him.

"And that's why you look like a marshmallow combatant?" Cole asked me and smiled. "I have to go but wish me luck!"

"You don't need it, but good luck," I said to him, giving his hand a reassuring squeeze.

Cole turned and continued away from me as I went to resume my hiding position. By the time I got back into position, he was emerging from the trees with his helmet on, but I would know his figure anywhere. I watched him pick up a bow and fiddle with it a few times. It was not his choice of weapon at all, but he was probably a decent enough shot.

He impressed me by putting an arrow in each of the six standstill targets, but had a bit more trouble with the moving ones. I could see him as he moved his arm from side to side trying to decide where to go with his shots. His hesitation caused his shots to miss their targets and he only landed three more arrows, giving him a total of nine out of fifteen. Oliver's total had been thirteen which was probably going to be the number to beat.

I heard Cole coming back through the trees to where I was hiding. He stopped below me and looked up at me.

"There was a lot more pressure knowing I was going up against the best wielder that the ORC has," he said from below me with a smile.

"You did fine!" I called down to him.

"Thanks, Lex. When it's your turn, knock 'em dead," Cole said. He headed away from me and I was left in my tree alone again.

Vic appeared next, landing a total of nine arrows followed by Greg who landed ten arrows and then finally Fitz came running through the trees. He stood in the area under my hiding spot and I dropped down next to him, surprising him so much that he threw himself sideways.

"Geez Lex!" He cried out. "How are you? Ready?"

"Better now that I'm out of that tree," I answered, stretching my back and my arms out. "How did this morning go?"

"Really great!" Fitz answered. "I managed to bring Cole down and he's one of the best fighters I've ever seen. I used all of your moves you taught me, otherwise I would've been on my ass in a second."

For half a second, I was surprised at him saying he beat Cole, but then I remembered Cole was going to throw his performance. I was eager to hear all about how it went this morning and I knew that if I got a chance to talk to Cole, he would spare me no details.

I put my hair up on top of my head so it didn't spill out from beneath the helmet and give me away. I held my hand out for the helmet from Fitz.

"Good luck, Lexi," he said and handed it to me.

"Thanks, Fitz. It'll be okay and you'll be a great leader when this is all done," I answered and put the helmet on top of my head, tucking my stray hairs up in it.

"I really owe you," Fitz said.

"Yes you do, but you also really need to hide in case someone comes," I said and gave him a little push to climb the tree that I had just vacated.

I headed to the spot I was to emerge from with my helmet on. The headpiece was slightly heavy and a little uncomfortable but nothing I couldn't bear for the next few minutes. I was just hoping it didn't throw off my aim.

I emerged from the trees and took a breath in, thankful that the helmet left me some room to breathe. There was one bow and one full quiver left for me and I tossed it on my back and picked up the bow. It was made out of stained wood and it was smooth between my fingers. It was probably the nicest bow I had ever held.

I pulled an arrow out and nocked it against the string, pulling it taut. With the helmet on, I couldn't press my thumb to my cheek so I rested it on the helmet and took some steadying breaths while I waited for the whistle to signal me to start.

As soon as that high pitched whistle sounded, I let my arrow fly. It landed on the first target, but not in the center and I knew I had to make a slight adjustment to compensate for this new bow and for my thumb placement due to my helmet. I rapidly fired five more arrows, putting one in the center of each target and arming myself with another one, waiting for the targets to start moving.

Right on cue, the recruits hiding behind them began to move with their large targets and I tracked the one on the far left with my eyes and fired, hitting it right in the center. I hit the next one and the next one as I sent arrows flying down the line and hit all six of the moving targets.

I grabbed another arrow and sent it towards the furthest back recruit who was backing up with their target trying to put space between themselves and my dangerous aim. It buried itself in the middle of the target and hit with such velocity that the recruit holding it tipped over backwards and the target laid flat on top of them. I could only see his feet sticking out.

I decided I was going to go big with my last two arrows so I pulled them both from my quiver and held them against the string. I moved my middle finger between them as I adjusted the angle that they were going to fly. When I was satisfied, I pressed my thumb to the side of my helmet and I let go, sending the two arrows flying away from me and away from each other.

They each hit their marks in two of the targets closer to the center and I smiled under my helmet. I slung the bow over my shoulder too and turned my back on the field and ducked back into the trees.

I kept my helmet on until I navigated my way back to where I left Fitz and I didn't say a word until he jumped down from the tree, indicating that the area was clear. I pulled the helmet straight up and off my head and took in a deep breath. I had sweat on my forehead and it had plastered some stray hairs to my face.

"That. Was. Epic," Fitz said and he wrapped his arms around me in a bear hug, pinning my arms to my sides as he lifted me off the ground.

"No problem," I answered when he finally put me down and I could breathe again. I handed him back the helmet and started immediately removing the layers of clothing that were bulking me up until I got to my simple wardrobe at the base of my layers. I hid the clothes back in the hollow of the tree, where I would return for them later when there were less eyes on this area.

"Just wow! I can't believe how good you were!" Fitz said excitedly.

"Just remember that was you, so you need to act like it," I reminded him. "You should probably put the helmet on for a bit so it messes up your hair and looks believable. Oh, and take the bow because I accidentally left the field with it."

I handed over the bow and the quiver, which he slung over his shoulder awkwardly. We would have to work on that too.

"Got it. Thanks again, Lexi," Fitz said before putting the helmet on and heading away from me.

I quickly adjusted my hair, making it look a little neater and wiping some more of the sweat off of my face as I headed back. As much as I loathed Nate, I couldn't deny that he had skills and he taught me everything that I know, making me quite the Wielder that I was today.

I ran into Ellis on my journey back to our quarters and we walked the last distance together.

"Sorry I missed you," Ellis said, "I got hung up and then was afraid that I'd run into you know who. How did it go?"

"They had to wear these helmets so you didn't know who was who," I explained, playing a little dumb.

"Did you know which one was Cole? How did he do?" she asked quietly.

"I would always know him, helmet or not," I answered honestly. "He did okay, he hit nine targets but someone else hit thirteen and then the last guy hit all fifteen."

"Wow! All fifteen? That's impressive. I would love to know who that was!" Ellis squealed. "Surely they'll announce it at the party tonight."

"So is the party just like the dinner? Keep the wine coming and the guests happy?" I asked her with a smile.

"Basically! We will probably just be serving champagne to the guests. Usually King Joseph will even let us have a glass or two, but any more than that and you'll find me asleep in a corner," Ellis said with a laugh.

"Oh believe me, I have been there," I said, remembering my experience when I drank nearly an entire bottle of wine and almost died.

I held the door for Ellis as she and I went inside the castle. The rest of my new friends were all inside and asked us about updates on the competition. We shared our limited knowledge and spent some time relaxing and swapping tales before it was time to get ready for the party that would likely start in a few hours.

17

The party was running smoothly as Ellis and I weaved our way between the many members of the M.A. that were in the great room. A few new recruits and seasoned members opted out of the festivities to keep watch on the kingdom while the rest celebrated the announcement of the newest Rank Leaders, which was any moment now.

King Joseph was present and he was dressed in a formal navy blue suit, complete with a neatly pressed tie. Fitz was dressed similarly. Most of the men were wearing suits and if they weren't, they still had classy jacket and pant combinations donned for the occasion. Ellis and I had on our usual ensemble and did not look quite as formal as the rest of the guests at the party.

But it was the fanciest I had ever felt. I realized that I might have had a very different upbringing if that fire never happened as a child. Perhaps fancy parties would have been my normal, along with long gowns and men in suits.

Cole had found me the second that he entered the room. His green eyes sought me out and I had maneuvered my way to him with a champagne glass ready in my hand.

Under the guise of small talk about the party, Cole had told me all of the details from this morning about the combat part of the competition. He said that Fitz performed really well but so did Oliver. Oliver's performance in both demonstrations were strong so it would likely be a close call and we still didn't know how many of these new leaders the King would choose. I had hoped that my weapons performance was enough to give Fitz the edge over Oliver.

I watched Oliver steal glances at Ellis occasionally but he never approached her. She and I had agreed before the party started that I would stick close to him so that she could keep a safe distance from him.

I estimated that there were likely one hundred people in the great room for this party, and almost exclusively all were M.A. members, with the exception of us staff members.

Brooke had whipped up some appetizers that were passed around by Thomas and Rita on large silver trays to the guests and everyone seemed to be enjoying themselves. There was soft music being played on stringed instruments in the corner of the large space and I wondered how these types of events looked back home in Odessa compared to here.

The music began to quiet down and I noticed that King Joseph took his place at the head of the room on a small platform that stood there. There was a podium on the platform but he stood next to it rather than behind it. He unclasped his hands and held them out to indicate that he requested quiet from the crowd.

"Good evening all!" King Joseph announced. "Thank you all for coming, and congratulations on all of the impressive performances today. I am excited for another wave of recruits to be added in order to strengthen our forces, and equally excited to see who has emerged as the most qualified from our performances today."

The King paused for a moment.

"If the five competitors could assemble up here with me, please," he requested.

Slowly, the five competitors made their way to the front and stood shoulder to shoulder, proud and tall, on the floor in front of the King.

"As you all can see, my son, Prince Joseph is eligible for the position so he performed today with these gentlemen, but in order to be fair, they performed with helmets on so that they could not be identified by their faces. The best competitors must be selected for the roles to best lead their fellow army mates and protect the kingdom."

I listened to King Joseph talk for a while as he went on about honor and loyalty and spoke of the previous members of the M.A. who have made the organization proud. I looked around the room at everyone with their eyes trained on the King in the front of the room and thought about how Cole and I were likely going to move on from this place very soon. We did our part to find each other and help Fitz and now we had to continue our journey to find Remy.

I spotted Ellis on the other side of the room mirroring my location towards the back corner. Even with a tray of full champagne glasses in one hand, she lifted the other to give me a slight wave and a thumbs up. I would miss her when we left but hopefully I could pass through this place again and perhaps she and I could stay in touch as long as no one finds out I am a wanted fugitive.

"My staff, Rita, helped me to determine who is most fit to be in the leadership position. I spoke with Rita and instructed her with my thoughts and we devised a ranking system to score the performers. Rita, if you will," the King said and waved her forward.

My eyes found her moving through the crowd with a light blue envelope in her small hands. She had abandoned her tray somewhere and held the envelope in two hands as she made her way to the stage. She gave a slight bow of the head to King Joseph and handed him the envelope before receding into the crowd of M.A. members.

I watched as King Joseph slid his thumb under the seal of the envelope and opened it, removing the paper that was inside it. He was definitely moving slowly on purpose to create suspense in the room.

"It is my pleasure to announce that we will have two Army Rank Leaders joining the ranks and they are... Joseph and Oliver!"

Thunderous applause filled the room as people clapped and cheered for the newest army officials. The men at the front all shook hands, exchanged back slaps and congratulated the newly appointed leaders.

I let out a breath at the news that it wasn't Cole. Even though he said he wasn't going to accept the position if he was awarded it, I knew that would be a struggle for him since he liked to prove himself and take on challenges head first. He knew that we were getting ready to move on though.

But Fitz would be a great leader, since he listened to others and understood people. Oliver would probably be more of the muscle and the military mind with his personality. I hoped that they would make a good team and be able to shape the new recruits into decent and efficient members. The kingdom of Middletown seemed like a nice place.

I looked back over to Ellis and noticed that she was no longer standing where she had been. Perhaps the news about Oliver had upset her and she needed a minute to gather her thoughts. I continued across the room heading in her general direction when the rear doors at the back of the hall burst open, nearly hitting me in the face. I took a step back behind the door, thankful I didn't drop my tray of champagne, although it only had one glass on it and surveyed the tall individual dressed in all black who appeared in the doorway.

I was immediately drawn to the singular colored golden yellow embroidered band around their sleeve, in addition to the sleek bow and arrow that was secured to his back. As I peered out from behind the door, the flash of red hair was impossible to miss and I realized that my worst nightmare was coming true.

Nate Hogan was here.

18

Nate stood in the entranceway to the great room, not even five feet from me. I held my breath as I looked around the room waiting for the M.A. members to jump into action and attack or arrest this intruder. But no one was overly concerned by him bursting through the door.

"Nathaniel!" King Joseph boomed and stepped down off of the platform with opened arms. "It's so good to see you again!"

"Your Majesty, the pleasure is mine," Nate answered and bowed low to the King.

I watched Cole use the moment that Nate's head was down to slide silently out of the room before he returned to a standing position.

"Please come in! You've returned on a perfect day. We've just chosen two new Rank Leaders, my son Joseph and Oliver here," King Joseph announced and waved Nate further into the room.

Nate walked up the middle of the room, tall and proud towards the King and the newest leaders of the M.A. He gave a strong handshake to King Joseph first and then to Fitz and Oliver. The King ushered them towards the side of the room towards the door that Cole had just snuck out of but I stayed hidden for now.

"Please, all, continue to enjoy the party! Excuse us for a moment," King Joseph said and exited through the side door with the three men in tow.

I let out a sigh of relief as the sounds of the party picked up again. I picked up the champagne tray and downed the last glass I had remaining on it. Leaving the empty glass on a table, I held my tray close to my face in case I had to cover myself if Nate appeared.

It would be disastrous to be spotted by him.

I swiftly exited through the doors that Nate had entered through and peered around the corner looking for the rest of his team or my team, or any team. The fact that he entered here alone, was not searched or attacked, and no one seemed concerned at his arrival could only mean one thing.

Nate was known by people here, especially the King. And if that was the case, then he had to be some sort of spy for the M.A.

I had to figure out why he was here so I snuck down the hallway and around the great room towards where they had exited. I knew these halls pretty well now and I could likely get there and not be spotted.

My steps were slow and deliberate on the carpeted floors as I listened fiercely for any sounds of their conversation. I was almost to the end of the hallway when I finally caught a hint of a male timbre speaking. I followed the sounds to a closed door which I knew to be one of the many offices in this place.

I stood outside of the closed door, concentrated on the conversation on the other side of the wall and listened.

"How is the mission going?" King Joseph asked. "Have you been able to get close to the son?"

"Sort of, sir," Nate answered. "We work on the same team and were sent out on a mission together."

"So you haven't befriended him yet and he doesn't trust you completely?" King Joseph asked again. There was a tone of annoyance in his voice.

"I'll do you one better, sir," Nate replied. "I know you wanted me to get close to Damion in order for him to put me in the Queen's pocket. He and I are cordial. But Queen Camilla and I... we are very close. She trusts me completely and has me on a special mission currently."

"My boy!" King Joseph exclaimed and I heard what sounded like him clapping Nate on the back.

"What is this secret mission that you are on?" I heard Oliver ask.

"There are two fugitives that escaped from Odessa and she has me tracking them down. Both are former, now disgraced ORC members and get this, one is Princess Alexandria, the girl who was thought to have died in the fire. She's alive, fooled us all, joined the ORC, and now she's gone rogue," Nate explained.

Rogue! I felt my skin turn hot at Nate's lies about how I was a fugitive. I was also so angry at myself for trusting him and befriending him during ORC training, now that I knew that he truly was a spy sent to Odessa to get close to Damion and Camilla. He truly had us all fooled, even the Queen.

"Princess Alexandria is alive?" King Joseph asked. "Is she dangerous?"

"Yes," Nate answered, "but nothing I can't handle. Queen Camilla has given me new orders to bring her in alive. I can't imagine her getting this far, she was injured pretty badly."

"How badly?" Fitz asked.

"She has scars up and down her back and arms from that fire as a child but those are healed. She took a stab wound to the leg recently, but knowing her, she treated her own injury. She has skills in three of the four divisions of the ORC: Combatants, Wielders, and the Medics, so she shouldn't be underestimated," Nate explained.

I closed my eyes at the mention of my scars. I don't think any of the men in that room had seen my scars except for Fitz and hopefully he wouldn't be able to put the information together.

"Their Wielders are their weapons experts, right?" I heard Fitz ask. "What is Alexandria's weapon of choice?"

"Bow and arrow," Nate answered. "Unfortunately, she is an excellent shot."

"So is my son! He hit all of the targets, even the moving ones during the competition today. She would be no match for him!" King Joseph said enthusiastically.

I knew with that revealing information that there was no way that Fitz didn't know. He had to be putting the pieces together.

"Excuse me," I heard Fitz say and then footsteps approached the door where I was standing.

I moved with speed, ducked around the corner and ran down the hall before opening a door and stepping into one of the interior stairwells. If Fitz knew, he had just chosen to not tell anyone in that room but he could at any moment.

I climbed the staircase and headed for Fitz's training room where I could at least arm myself with a bow and maybe a few knives, in case Nate found out I was here and I had to fight my way out.

It was slightly reassuring that he said Camilla had now wanted me to come in alive rather than be killed by Nate somewhere out here. At least I knew now that his shots were not meant to kill... hopefully.

I opened the door at the top of the stairwell and peeked down the hall. It was silent and empty. I quickly moved through the doorway and down the wide hallway, constantly throwing looks over my shoulder as I went. I opened the door to the library and made my way over to the part of the bookcase that would swing away and let me into the training room.

It did just that and I stepped into the training room and closed the door behind me, sealing myself inside. I let out a breath of air, quickly changed out of my dress and into the more practical training clothes that Fitz had left for me. I crossed the room to the weapons wall where I strapped a full quiver to my back and assessed the bows hanging from the wall before selecting one that had a smooth wood finish.

"Lexi..." a voice said from behind me.

I had the bow in my hand already and spun with it, drawing an arrow from my quiver in a flash and pulling it taut as I eyed the person that said my name.

I looked down my arrow into Fitz's dark brown eyes as he looked back at me over the gun in his hand. I had looked down its barrel once before on our first night here when we cornered during the celebration in the town.

His hands were shaking slightly but I could tell that he was much more familiar with this weapon than with the bow that we had been practicing with.

"Lexi..." Fitz repeated. "Put that down."

"You know I'm a better shot than you," I said to him. "You first."

"The dart will fire out of here at twice the speed your arrow will and I probably won't miss from this distance," Fitz answered, not taking his eyes off of me.

"What do you want, Fitz?" I asked him, my thumb lightly resting on my cheek. If he made any sudden moves, I was prepared to alter the trajectory of my arrow and sink it into his leg rather than his chest but he stood there unmoving except for the occasional nervous tremor in his hand.

"You... you're from Odessa, aren't you?" Fitz asked, the nervousness now apparent in more than just his hands. "You're Princess Alexandria."

I didn't answer right away. I was weighing the best course of action that I could take knowing that Fitz was definitely going to believe Nate and his father over me.

"By birth, yes," I answered. "I only learned this very recently and I know what Nate told you, but, I promise I am not a fugitive."

"How do you know what Nate told me?" Fitz asked.

"When the man who has tried to kill you twice, once out of jealousy and once just because, shows up where you are, you find out why. I heard him telling you about his mission. I had a feeling you were going to figure it out when he described my scars," I explained.

"He's tried to kill you twice?" Fitz said.

"The first time, he set my cabin on fire and locked me and my sister inside, and then he stabbed me and left me to bleed out but C--, someone came along and saved me, thankfully," I answered. I decided to leave Cole out of my tale to keep him safe.

"That doesn't mean you aren't a criminal!" Fitz said and his hands were really shaking now.

"Fitz," I said calmly, trying to diffuse the situation. I softened my hold on the bow and lowered the arrow slightly in good faith. I sighed before continuing.

"Yes, I am Alexandria, but I've always been Lexi. I am in the ORC, or I was. It's complicated when your own mother is trying to kill you. I left Odessa to get away from Nate and just stumbled upon Middletown, just like how I stumbled upon you on my first day here. I do have a skill-set, as you are aware, but I grew up that way so I could always protect myself if I needed to. Nate is really dangerous, Fitz. His only agenda is for himself."

"It seems like he did his part infiltrating the ORC really well," Fitz said coldly and my heart sank that he didn't believe me. "I... I can't let you leave here, Lexi."

"I have to go," I said to him and I slowly pulled my arrow taut again. "There are other people that I need to find, like my friends and my family."

"I have a job as a Rank Leader now. I have to protect this kingdom and its people. So you can't leave," Fitz said.

"I'll either go around you or through you, Fitz. I don't want to hurt you but I--."

Pew! Pew!

Suddenly, I crumbled to the ground as my leg gave out from under me. I had a stinging pain in my leg and looked down to see a small cylindrical shaped dart sticking out of my thigh. A quick spin of my head saw the other dart in the wall behind me.

I looked up at Fitz as he crossed the room towards me on the ground with his weapon still pointed at me as I plucked the dart from my thigh. It wasn't pain like when Nate had stabbed me in the other leg but it had quite a sting to it. The sensation traveled down my leg as I realized that I couldn't move my leg no matter how much I willed it.

"Fitz, what did you do?" I yelled at him, obviously losing my cool. My fingers started to tingle as I held onto my bow loosely.

"I can't trust you right now, Lexi, not until I have all of the answers," Fitz explained to me. "It's a mild sedative so you should lose sensation and then basically fall asleep."

"You hit me with a tranq dart?" I asked angrily. I pulled my bow back with my arrow still in it, and although I wobbled a bit, I pressed my tingling thumb to my face, blew out air through pursed lips and sent an arrow right at Fitz's small weapon.

My aim was true, hitting the small gun, startling him as my arrow ricocheted off and clipped his hand, causing him to drop the gun as it skidded towards me. My leg that I plucked the dart out of was fast asleep, so I used the odd numbness I could feel starting to grow in my other leg to push off of the wall and send myself towards Fitz's gun. He was grabbing his hand and I could see a small amount of blood dripping where I nicked him with my arrow but he was not looking at me.

I fumbled my hands around his weapon, pointed it at him, pretending that it was like any weapon that Remy had taught me to use as an extension of my hand and pulled the trigger twice.

Pew! Pew!

Fitz stared at me and then at the two darts I put right in his torso through his fancy shirt. He probably regretted crossing the room to get closer to me now. If he had remained on the other side, I probably would have missed him. I could be a decent shot at this close range, like when I hit Brayden with the paint gun what seems like years ago during ORC training.

"Sorry about your shirt," I said as he fell to his knees. I was taking slow, deep breaths and willing myself to stay awake despite how tired I felt.

Fitz tipped over onto his side and then rolled onto his back. He tried to move his hands towards his chest to pull the darts out but he was moving too slow and his arms collapsed at his sides.

"Pull them out?" he asked me.

I didn't answer but looked at him laying on the ground only about two feet from me.

"The longer they're in, the more medication gets delivered. I think that's why you didn't pass out yet," Fitz said through gritted teeth. "Most people don't think about removing them."

"I'm not most people," I said, dangerously and looked at him lying on the ground with the two darts in his chest. They likely had been in long enough to keep him down, I assumed.

"Are you going to shoot me again?" I asked him as I pulled my upper body towards him. My legs were both hardly working right now.

He didn't answer but shook his head.

"I can still shoot you with something you can't pluck out of your skin so easily... so don't make me regret this," I said as I reached over and plucked both darts from his torso and dropped them on the floor behind me.

Fitz let out a long breath but didn't make any moves towards me. In fact, he was quiet for the next ten minutes or so and I took the time to relax and try to think about what to do next.

I assumed Cole was doing what I was doing, getting himself together so we could run at the next opportunity that presented itself. I was hoping to pack some weapons from this room, some food from the kitchen, my small amount of possessions from my room in the staff quarters and then run with Cole.

I was starting to be able to move my toes and the tingling was going away in my upper body although it was slow progress. Fitz was still not moving on the ground although he was breathing normally so it startled me when he spoke.

"If you want to tell me your side of things, I'll listen," he said although he did not turn his head to me.

"Because you can't move and want to pass the time?" I asked with a hint of attitude.

"Even with one dart, you shouldn't have had as much movement as you had and even now, I can hear you moving. Look at me, it's taking all of my energy to not just pass out right now and it was like you hardly got hit," Fitz explained.

I did pull my dart out rather quickly, but I felt it working the second after it had pierced my skin.

"Plus, you've had multiple opportunities to... to kill me since the moment we met and even now in this room and you didn't take them. Even after I called you out, and shot you." He paused. "And yes, we are both stuck here until the med wears off and we can actually move again. I'm no threat to you now."

"Speak for yourself, Fitz," I said quietly but his words were true. Perhaps he was starting to trust me or really did want to hear my story.

"I'll listen, Lexi," Fitz said sincerely.

I decided to tell Fitz my tale of how I got here. I left out Remy and Cole's names to keep them safe but surely if he knew I was Alexandria then he knew who my siblings were, so I included them.

I told him of ORC training, of the people I met, and all about Nate. I recounted the cabin fire, escaping with my sister and returning to the castle to be blindsided by his allegiance to the Queen and to learn of her distaste for me, her seemingly unwanted child.

I skipped the part about my first mission to Remy's house where the realization had hit me but I included the part about being made to do whatever the Queen said in order to guarantee my sister's safety when I was on the mission.

I relived the story of Nate stabbing me in the woods and I rubbed my leg where I knew the faint scar was hiding underneath my pant leg. I told Fitz of the friend who had rescued me, continuing to leave Cole's name out and then told him we had been separated before arriving in Middletown and I was hoping to find him.

"Nate isn't a good person, or he hasn't been to me or my friends," I said. "If he is here, I can't be. So I have to go and find my friends."

Fitz was silent and I desperately hoped he didn't fall asleep during my tale because I didn't want to have to tell it again.

"I think I believe you," Fitz said quietly and rotated his head to face me.

I whipped my head in his direction and felt a few tears brewing behind my eyes.

"Fugitives, criminals, bad people. They don't do what you did to help me, they don't make connections or befriend people and they certainly don't take a job in the castle, actually do the job and do it well," he said and I felt the first tear slip out. "I can tell you mean me or any-one here no harm."

I had a few tears falling and they did not help me keep up my threatening and dangerous appearances.

"I'm sorry I shot you," Fitz added. "Guess you're lucky that I'm a lousy shot with that too." Now he added a smile.

I cracked a smile too. A small one.

"Your team that you set out with... the one with your siblings on it?" Fitz asked.

"Yeah?" I replied.

"I'm pretty sure that they're here," Fitz answered.

"What?!" I yelled and pulled myself up next to Fitz. I was almost back at one hundred percent and at my norm before Fitz shot me.

He flinched a little as I moved so abruptly towards him but he was still not able to move anything other than his head.

"The way you described them made me think of these intruders that the M.A. snatched up the other day. They've been kept here for questioning," Fitz said.

"The other day? How many days? And who knows that they're here?" I demanded.

"After the break in at the Lodge, we upped the security and extended our perimeter otherwise we would've never found them sneaking around on the outskirts. They had clothes similar to what Nate was dressed in when he walked in with those embroidered sleeves," Fitz said.

My heart sank and I knew it had to be my team. But if they were being held here for questioning, it meant that they were in the castle and I could get them out. I wondered if Nate turned them over to the M.A. or how he managed to convince them to come this way. I had a lot of questions and I knew that I wouldn't get the answers that I needed or wanted from Fitz.

"I need you to take me there," I said to Fitz.

He lifted his head off of the ground a little bit and moved his eyes towards his feet which remained unmoving.

"I need a little bit of time, here," he said and then looked back at me, indicating his body was still not ready to move.

I rolled to my hands and knees and pushed myself up onto my feet, giving them a firm push into the ground to make sure I had my feeling back in them.

"I've never seen anybody combat the effects of the darts that fast," Fitz said from the floor.

"You never told me that you guys use guns," I said to him and crossed my arms.

"They don't shoot anything deadly, thankfully. Tranquilizer darts, small pellets that don't penetrate skin, they just hurt like something fierce. They honestly look like modified toys or something. And obviously, my aim continues to be terrible."

I scooped up the one I had shot out of Fitz's hand. The handle was partially bent from it hitting the floor, and it was a miracle that my shots hit their target. I checked the quiver on my back to ensure it was still full and in place and held the bow in my hand.

"I'm going to get some things together," I said. "Be back soon."

"I'll be here," Fitz answered sarcastically as he put his head back on the floor and continued to look at the ceiling.

I slipped out the training room door back into the library and out into the hallway. I crept along the wall and traced my steps back to the staircase I had taken earlier to find my way to the second floor as I needed to now get back down to the main floor. My goal was to find the cellar that they had told me they used for a dungeon weeks ago on my own, in case Fitz was not to be trusted and was luring me there as a trap.

I opened the stairwell door and emerged into another empty hallway. Silence greeted me as I headed back the way that I came, hoping to find the entrance to the cellar. I was going off my memories of the maps Ellis had drawn for me, and I remembered a few unmarked doors that were near the entrance to the staff quarters.

I turned the last corner and could hear the sounds of the party still in full swing so I kept going past the event and towards the staff entrance.

The double wooden doors that marked the entrance to the space I called home for the past several weeks opened slowly as I approached. I secured my arrow and pulled back, taking aim from one of my knees in an alcove off the side of the hallway.

A small figure in a blue dress emerged from the opening with her hands clenched at her sides. Her eyes were down and her familiar perfectly positioned bun was angled towards me with her head pointed down.

"Ellis," I whispered, not putting my arrow down.

Her head tipped up slowly and she looked around, her eyes unable to find me but showing recognition of my voice.

"Where are you?" she asked.

I took a breath and extended to my regular height and although I kept my arrow in my bow, I did aim it away from my friend as I stepped into the hallway.

"Lexi," she breathed a sigh of relief at seeing me and then her expression changed. "What the heck are you doing? And what are you doing with that?" She gestured at the bow and arrow then put her fists in her pockets.

"I haven't been totally honest with you, Ellis," I said to my friend. "I have a few more skills than just what you saw between Oliver and I. I didn't tell you because I thought it would keep you safer."

"Keep me safe from what?" she asked as she came closer to me.

"My goal was always to get in, find Cole, and get out, as you know. He and I aren't from here and there are dangerous people after us. People close to me could be used as leverage to get me to do what they want," I explained and I looked at the ground. "And it's been done before by using my own twin sister against me."

"So it is true," Ellis whispered.

"What is?" I asked.

"You *are* the princess from Odessa," she whispered to me.

My eyes got wide at the revelation of information coming from Ellis that she should not know. I took a slight step back from her, keeping my hands on my weapon in case I had to use it although it would be a challenge for me to ever hurt Ellis.

"Oliver told me," Ellis said, her eyes cast down. "I left the party after the announcement because I needed a minute. He and that new guy came to find me and warn me about you. They asked me where you were. I obviously didn't know so I left them and here I am now."

"Ellis, you can't believe what they say about me. I promise I'm nothing like they make me out to be," I said, wary of the door behind her in case they were still in the staff quarters.

"I don't believe them. You've been nothing but kind since you arrived, although a little secretive but we all have our secrets. They said you would try to kill me or anyone who got in your way, and honestly, if that was the case, you're the worst criminal ever because you had so many times to kill me and somehow, you still haven't."

I smiled at Ellis because Fitz had said the same thing to me upstairs. Then I remembered I left him lying on the ground up there and I was on a mission to find my friends in the so-called dungeon.

"Ellis, I need your help," I said and took a step closer to her again.

The hallway around us remained quiet as she closed the gap between us, causing me to lower my weapon.

"Wait. Oliver gave me these," she said at a super low whisper and reached into her dress pockets and pulled out two darts identical to what Fitz had shot me with earlier. "Told me to uncap it and... and..." her voice faded away and she struggled to regain it. She leaned in right in front of me and finished, "And stab you with them."

Ellis had tears freely falling from the corners of her eyes as she continued to hold the darts out to me. I took them from her and pocketed them before taking her hands in mine.

"That was really brave of you," I said to her. "Thank you for trusting me enough to not stab me with those. They're... unpleasant."

"It's not like you'd ever been hit with one before, right?" Ellis asked.

I opened my mouth to answer her honestly for once when the double doors that Ellis had come through burst open aggressively. The flash of light red hair sent my heart rate soaring as I grabbed Ellis and spun her behind me and pulled my arrow taut, aiming it right at...

"Oliver," I said, eyeing him down the shaft of my arrow.

Oliver stood there with open arms and a terrible gleam in his eyes as the doors swung shut behind him.

"Imagine my surprise when I learn that you, of all people, are one of the fugitives from Odessa. No wonder you know how to fight. You are former and now disgraced Odessa Royal Command," Oliver said to me.

I fired my arrow and planted it in the ground probably less than an inch from the tip of his shoe and had another one ready to go instantaneously. Ellis let out a little gasp from behind me.

"Ellis, she's dangerous. Get away from her!" Oliver called.

"She's my friend!" Ellis shouted back at Oliver, and he stayed where he was.

He put his hands up to show that he wasn't armed but I didn't trust him still and by the look on his face, the feeling was mutual.

"Ellis," I said quietly to the girl crouched behind me. "Go, in case this gets ugly. Now."

I heard her mumble some sort of version of "Okay" and heard her shuffle away from the current standoff at our end of the hallway but I didn't stop glaring at Oliver. Taking my eyes off of him could prove deadly.

"What's your play here, Alexandria?" Oliver asked, taking a step over the arrow I shot. "The entire M.A. is in that room for the party and one call will bring them all running."

"I'm going to leave, whether you get in my way or not," I answered. "You wouldn't be the first person I've shot today." I watched a little bit of the color drain from his face at my comment, which wasn't technically untrue.

His grimace turned into a terrible smile and he put his hands down.

"You better put those back where I can see them," I said, nodding my head at him.

"You better put that weapon down, Little Lexi," a cold voice said from behind me, "and turn around."

My breath caught and I froze as I recognized the voice immediately, especially by the taunt that was thrown in there.

"I might just shoot Oliver first and then turn around and shoot you next, Nate. The payback for my stab wound would be nice," I answered, trying to keep my cool.

"You wouldn't risk firing anything at me," Nate said.

"Oh yeah?" I half snarled, keeping my eyes on Oliver.

"Lexi..." Ellis' voice squeaked, causing me to spin immediately towards her voice.

Nate had his left arm around her neck and was holding a very sharp blade poised right next to her throat. She had her arms up and was pulling on his arm but her strength was no match for his, which I knew from experience.

I threw a look back at Oliver and he hadn't moved, but I could see his eyes had a small amount of concern in them, as if he was hoping that Nate didn't hurt her. I knew that he cared about her by just looking at him, but his actions when he and I squared off in the forest by the Lodge said otherwise.

"Nate, let her go," I said to my enemy and I adjusted my trajectory towards his face, which was the only part of him not really covered by Ellis' body.

"I taught you how to use that, Lexi. You know I could put her body in front of your shot just as quickly," Nate countered. "And she'll die."

Ellis whimpered and twisted her small frame, trying to get out of Nate's grip but her efforts were useless.

"Or you don't put that down, and I cut her, and she still dies," he said.

I stayed where I was. Oliver was still rooted to where he was and Nate and Ellis stayed where they were for a good minute.

"Time is ticking," Nate said and he flicked the blade. Ellis let out a little scream and I saw a drop of red start to slide down her neck where he flicked her with the sharp end of his knife.

"Okay, okay! Nate!" I called. I reluctantly released the tension in my bow, and held my arrow in my left hand.

"Put it down," Nate commanded and I lowered the arrow to the floor.

I was moving to put my bow on the floor with my other hand when Ellis cried out, "Lexi!"

I looked up at her as Nate took the handle of the blade and smacked her in the temple. She crumbled to the ground, her hands on her head and rolled from her back to her side with a groan.

I moved quickly to pick up my arrow as she shouted my name when I felt someone's presence behind me. I was too slow to react and I felt the familiar double sting of two darts right in the side of my neck. I threw up my hands to pull them out but was tackled and thrown forward with my arms underneath my body.

"Lexi!" Ellis screamed again.

Strong hands rolled me onto my back and I felt those darts working so much faster this time into my neck by Oliver. My head lolled to the side and I saw Ellis' fearful face.

"You'll be... okay," I said to her trying to fight off the sedative.

"You won't be," Nate said to me and kicked my bow and arrow far enough away from me so that I couldn't reach them.

I tried to move my arm to reach out to Ellis but my arm didn't move. I wanted to let her know that everything would be fine even if I didn't entirely believe it. She looked down at her shaking hands, covered in blood from her head and neck wounds, both courtesy of Nate.

I watched Oliver walk over to her and she shooed him away, trying to crawl back away from him. She tossed one last look at me that was full of concern and sadness.

"You'll be okay too," she mouthed at me as Oliver gripped her arms and pulled her to her feet against her will. She fought back against him but he was able to easily overpower her.

I mustered enough strength to nod my head at her while she was still in my line of sight and then I closed my eyes, letting the sedative take over.

19

I woke up in very different surroundings than I had passed out in. The ground I was laying on was exceptionally hard, much harder than the carpeted hallway I had been laying on. It was also cold and damp.

I guess I had completed my own mission by finding the dungeon after all.

I couldn't be sure how much time had passed and I hoped Ellis was safe and that Fitz had earned his movements back. It certainly was an eventful party after all.

I rolled from my side to my back and let out a little groan at the pain that hit me in the side like someone had... hit me real good there.

"Lexi? Lexi, are you awake?" A feminine voice called and it echoed through wherever we were.

I groaned and finally opened my eyes and was staring at a cement ceiling. Great.

I was definitely in a cell. That much was evident by the cement and concrete surroundings, in addition to the walls of metal bars. Also great.

"Lexi? Are you okay?" The voice repeated.

I sat up, my ribs screaming in protest as I did so and even more so when I got to my feet and approached the bars to see who was calling me. I sure hoped Ellis was out there and might be able to spring me from here.

I leaned on the bars and gripped them with my hands, pulling and pushing to see if they'd budge, which they did not. The motion only aggravated my ribs more and I concluded that I must have been injured in what I assume was a rather ungraceful transfer to this prison.

Looking across the prison hallway to the cell on the other side, I saw a familiar and beautiful, although exceptionally dirty and bruised face.

"Ally," I breathed at the sight of my sister. "You're here." I finally analyzed her face as she pressed herself to the bars of her small cell. Her face was bruised in multiple places and she had a split lip although the blood appeared to have dried.

She smiled a big smile at me, and her lip split and a bit of blood rolled down her chin. She wiped it on her dirty sleeve, something the Ally I first met would never have done.

"Are you okay? You look..." I started.

"Badass? I thought so," she said and put her hands on her hips.

I laughed and pressed my hand to my abdomen where it hurt, and it stopped my laugh.

"Some redhead carried you down here and basically threw you in there. You didn't move so he kicked you... hard and more than once saying that it was payback.

Then you didn't move again until right now," Ally explained to me.

"How long was I out?" I asked.

"Probably a few hours or so. They took Damion as soon as they dropped you off," Ally answered.

Geez, a few hours or even more? I guess those darts are powerful when they're thrown directly into your bloodstream. Then I realized what she said about my brother.

"What do you mean, they took Damion?" I asked her.

"Oh you know, interrogation, questioning, punching practice," she answered and gestured to her face.

I was shocked at how calm and casual my sister was over all of this.

"Big Shot? Is that you over there?" A voice to my left called. I watched as a big figure appeared in the cell next to Ally's, looking worn and tired but not as injured as my sister was.

"Yager!" I said and grinned at the sight of him.

"Big Shot!" Yager yelled and banged on the bars. "I knew we'd find you! Brayden, look!"

Brayden's face appeared next to Yager's in the same cell. "Wow, Probie. Can't believe you left us to go chase Monahan alone," he said with a hint of sarcasm so I knew he wasn't truly mad.

I realized that my friends didn't know any of the truth. They probably thought Cole was still a criminal and on the run and I was chasing him. I ran my hands through my hair, thinking.

"Have you guys seen Nate?" I asked.

Ally shook her head.

"He went to scout ahead when we got close to this area and then we were attacked and brought here. But since he was looking ahead, he wasn't with us when they grabbed us. I just hope he wasn't caught. He's been a huge help getting us this far," she answered.

I clenched my fist. That was just like Nate - to lie and play his own agenda. I'm sure he knew that our team was here and was probably even responsible for it.

"Ally. Guys, listen to me. There's something that I need to tell you guys. It's about Nate, Cole, me and it's a lot but I need you to trust me," I said to my friends.

"Of course we trust you, Lexi," Ally said. "I'm just so glad we found you."

I took a breath in and out and steadied myself as I told my story, the entire story, from start to finish... again. This time was easier than when I told Fitz because I used everyone's names and didn't leave anything out. It helped that I was with these three in the ORC so I didn't have to recount too much of the middle section since they were there for it.

I picked up the tale around the time we left on the second mission to find Cole, and I had previously included all of his and the Queen's conversations that led up to that, the blackmail, as I was calling it, although it was more like coercion, and I closely monitored Ally's reactions to those parts of the tale. The fact that that was still her mother was not lost on me.

I jumped to the part where on our first night of our mission, I had eavesdropped on Nate, landing myself tied to a tree and bleeding to death in the forest when they all left to go and "find me." The fact that I had heard Ally call out for me and was able to reiterate her conversation with Nate helped make my story believable. As I spoke, I watched her eyes fill with sadness, belief, confusion, and recognition as she remembered the events exactly as I was telling them.

I told them about Cole's escape and his rescue of me and about our joint escape from our ORC pursuers until we got to Middletown. I finished up with everything else between then and how we got here to this exact point sitting in a cell. I spared no details about Nate threatening and hurting Ellis and told them all about those knockout darts that I had now been hit with three times.

I paused when I was finished and sat on the floor, tired from talking.

"You're telling us... hang on. I have too many questions and I don't know where to start," Brayden said and wrapped his hands around the bars to his and Yager's cell.

"Let's start with your attempted murder by Mum," Ally said quietly and put her back to the bars and me. She slid down them until she hit the ground. "I'm not sure I can believe it. It's Mum!"

I sighed, knowing that Ally was going to be the challenging one to convince.

"Camilla is so obsessed with power and I was a threat to that, so she decided to get rid of me. Fast forward fifteen years, when she learns that I'm alive and a human with feelings, so she can use me and as long as I do what she or my babysitter, Nate, said, she wouldn't harm you or Cole," I said.

"And she ordered a kill order for Nate to carry out?" Brayden asked, rubbing the back of head. He let out a low whistle. "Damn, Probie, that's low."

"He was almost successful if Cole hadn't shown up. I would be dead. I would've bled out, not fifty feet from where we had set up camp," I answered.

"How dare she!" Ally yelled and smacked her hand against the bars. "How dare she rob me of my sister growing up! Does she know I didn't leave that place for fifteen years? Does she know what it did to Damion, or what it did to our father? It destroyed all of us."

I wanted so badly to comfort my sister but with two sets of bars and several feet of space between us, it wasn't feasible. The best that could be done was Yager reaching through his bars to squeeze her arm, which he was currently doing to comfort her.

"So, where's Nate now?" Brayden asked.

"Somewhere in the castle, giving up any and all ORC information to King Joseph and the M.A." I answered, disappointedly.

"Not sure who's worse right about now, Queen Camilla for all the lies and attempted murder, or Nate for all the lies, attempted murder *and* espionage," Yager added.

"Definitely Nate," I said, looking at the ground.

The door at the end of the dimly lit cellar creaked open and there was a scuffling at the end of the hallway.

I got to my feet as Oliver and Vic appeared, both struggling to drag Damion down the concrete hallway to where we were located. He was half fighting them, half tripping over himself and his hands were tied in front of him.

"Put him in here," Oliver said to Vic as the two of them shoved my brother into the empty cell next to mine. He landed unceremoniously on the ground before they shut the cell door and double checked it was locked with a sharp pull.

Oliver stopped in front of my cell and looked at me through the bars and I glared back at him.

"This is a good look for you, Princess," he spat the last word at me. "Boy, does the King have plans for you."

I reached through the bars and tried to grab him but he stepped back and I swiped at air, feeling foolish for even trying.

He let out a roaring laugh and Vic chuckled by his side.

"Ellis is probably so disappointed in you," I said to him, hitting him where it hurts.

"You don't speak about her. And you won't ever see her again," Oliver said dangerously as he lowered his eyes at me.

He turned abruptly away from me and strode back down the hall with Vic in tow. I didn't speak until I heard the door creak open and close again.

"Damion?" I called as I ran to the side of my cell as close as I could get to him with the bars in the way. "It's me, Lexi. Are you alright?"

"Lexi?" he asked as he sat up and looked at me through two swollen black eyes.

"Geez, what did they do to you?" I said. "Is there information they need out of you that they can't get from Nate?"

"Nate?" Damion asked. "Dammit, did they get him too?"

A collective groan and a sigh went up as we realized we were going to have to repeat the tale for Damion and fill in the blanks for him.

I did so as quickly as I could, sitting on the ground in front of him as he sat close to me so I could untie the rope around his wrists. I had freed him long before I finished my tale, but he stayed that close to me and listened intently as I spoke.

"Mum?" he asked. "There's no way. It had to have been Cole and he's lying to you. Remember he knocked me out and escaped!"

I shook my head at my brother.

"Damion. I need you to trust me. She told Nate on the radio that night in the forest, Cole's story makes sense and it fits with mine and Remy's. I know how hard it is to believe, understand, comprehend, all of it!" I said to him, "Imagine how I feel, learning all of this after fifteen years, that I have siblings and a mother and a father. The excitement of knowing I have a real family, only to learn that she never wanted me and tried to kill me... multiple times."

Damion sat in silence. We all did.

"You used to be so close with Cole," I continued. "You know he doesn't have a bad bone in his body. You saw what he did for me that first day we met."

Damion flashed me a look, as we had an agreement to never discuss that, even to this day. So I didn't say more than that.

"He cares for you," Damion said quietly. "That much is obvious. But how can you say Mum doesn't?"

"She has ordered my death, sent Nate after me, sent more ORC guys after me, threatened me, you, Cole and Ally," I explained. "She has done nothing good and is just using me in whatever game she's playing."

"Damion, man," Brayden said from across the way. "I believe Lexi, I do. And you know her and I didn't see eye to eye when this all started, but she has all the pieces and they all fit together. If she was lying, well then damn because that's some story she's woven."

I gave Brayden a look of thanks for backing me up. I'm sure it would take Damion and Ally some time to accept the truth and come to terms with it. Ally seemed slightly more accepting, but still, it was her mother. I understood the hesitation.

There was more silence.

"So where's Cole?" Ally finally asked.

"I'm not sure. We were at a party and the second Nate arrived, we both slipped out opposite entrances of that room to not be seen by him. I'm not sure if Nate even knows that Cole is here. I haven't told any of the M.A. members who he is or even mentioned his name. The only saving grace is that Nate never said Cole's name in front of the other M.A. members when I was eavesdropping on them. But no promises that they don't know now," I said.

"If I know Cole, he'll soon know that you're down here and will come for you," Damion said.

I did know Cole and I knew he would do exactly that. I know that if he didn't find me soon, he would likely go to Ellis for help. Hopefully she was still on my side, after what Nate did to her and what she watched him and Oliver do to me.

"So what can we do now?" Ally asked.

"Anyone try breaking out yet?" I suggested as I got to my feet. "I know my way around this place, although this is the one place that I've never been to."

I put my hands on my hips, feeling the pain of where Oliver had kicked me in my ribs and feeling... something else. I unzipped my small jacket pockets and put my hands in them and wrapped my fingers around something small and slender.

A dart. No, wait. Two darts.

They were the ones that Ellis handed to me that I stowed in my pockets. They were small enough to be undetected, but it surprised me that they didn't pat me down before bringing me here. Nate knew I carried a knife most of the time, but without my ankle holster sitting obviously on my leg, he probably assumed I was unarmed.

"What's that?" Ally asked, eyeing me as I was examining the objects in my hand.

I looked up at her and smiled.

"This just might be our way out of here."

20

I had given Damion one of the darts and I held onto the other one deciding that if we got one of the M.A. members close enough to our cells, one of us would be able to grab them.

Damion recalled his story about when Cole grabbed him and used his own keys to escape from our home and told us that would be our best move. Cole had also told me that story so I already knew, but Damion painted Cole like a villain and when Cole told it, he came across like the hero. But it was in the past, so it didn't matter.

We waited for a while, hoping someone would come in to deliver water or food or something but no one came.

So we continued to wait.

We passed the time with the four of them filling me in on everything that had happened since the moment I "abandoned them" in search of Cole. They had said that Nate didn't act too strange, just overly concerned for my well-being and was slipping away occasionally. Brayden had said that he probably was communicating back with Camilla during those times.

Damion and Ally were coming around to the idea of Nate being the completely evil person I knew him to be, but they both weren't sold on Camilla yet. And I understood their reservations. If someone told me that Remy was "the bad guy," I'd tell them off right there.

I was hoping that the fact that Nate was here in Middletown and in this very castle, yet he had not come to try and rescue his team was earning me points in my favor and against him.

It had been a few hours since I had eaten and I was starting to feel worn down, so I assumed it was the middle of the night. If everyone was sleeping, it would make sense that we had no guests come to visit us.

I was sitting against the back wall of my cell with my arms crossed and my legs out straight in front of me. I had counted the number of bars on my cell about a thousand times. There were thirty eight of them, just standing there and keeping me inside and away from my friends, my family, and from Cole.

Just as I was about to close my eyes, I heard the quiet creak of the door opening at the end of the hall and slow, heavy footsteps.

I got to my feet and I heard Damion do the same in the cell beside me and we stood near the bars that divided us so that he and I could be closer together. I felt for the dart in my pocket and gave it a reassuring squeeze knowing that it was there.

Whoever was coming down the hall was certainly taking their sweet time, as minutes had passed before I even began to see a figure getting closer. The figure was tall, hunched over and exceptionally wide.

I felt my palms sweat at this new and approaching threat. If it was a person that large, I didn't think two darts would do the trick, especially since one dart didn't take me down completely and I wasn't a very big person.

"Lexi?" the voice whispered.

I couldn't recognize the timbre through the whispered tone, but it was familiar and male, and didn't give me chills like Nate did when he spoke so I risked a response.

"Who is it?"

"It's Fitz, where are you?" the voice replied.

"Fitz?" I asked and I wrapped my hands around the bars and pulled myself to the front of my cell.

Finally Fitz came into view and I realized why he was so hunched and wide. He had on two backpacks, had another two in his hand and a duffel bag in the other. He crouched down and placed them by the door of my cell and scanned the faces in each prison until he found me.

"You're okay," he said and walked towards me. I walked towards him too to keep him out of Damion's range so he didn't lunge early. I was curious why Fitz came all the way down here... it wasn't very glamorous for a prince.

"I got my movement back and then you didn't come back. I waited a bit and then went to look for you and it didn't take me long to find Nate, Oliver and you on the ground," Fitz continued.

"What happened when you got there?" I asked, mostly because I was just curious.

Fitz turned sideways and I saw that he had a quiver full of arrows and a bow slung across his back. Then he turned back to me, looking embarrassed.

"I panicked. I didn't want them to hurt you more but I also didn't want to lose my opportunity," Fitz said. "I told them you shot me, I mean, they could see the rips in my shirt. They really just put the rest of it together and I didn't have to say anything else. Oliver said he would bring you down here and leave you here until my father decided what he wanted to do."

"I'm sorry... your father?" Damion's angry voice interrupted. "Just who the hell are you?"

"Prince Joseph Fitzpatrick Cartwright," Fitz replied, "but my friends call me Fitz." He looked at me and winked as I remember him using that exact phrase when I formally met him.

"Lexi! Get away from him! He's one of them!" Damion shouted and launched himself at the bars between us. They obviously didn't budge.

"Damion, it's okay!" I said, trying to calm my brother before I turned back to Fitz. "We can trust him. He's not like Nate."

"Trust him? He came down here armed! Look!" Brayden said from across the way and pointed at the arrows on Fitz's back.

"I did," Fitz said, turning to face Brayden. "But these aren't for me. They're for you." The last part of that sentence was directed at me.

"For me?" I repeated, dumbly.

"This is the one you used during the Rank Leader's competition. I wanted you to have it," he replied and took it off of his shoulder and handed it to me through the bars. I took it wordlessly and put it around my shoulder and pulled the strap snug. "I didn't forget that I owe you one... or maybe two."

Fitz smiled and reached into his pocket and fished out a ring that had several keys on it. He fiddled with it for a while before he selected the one he wanted and inserted it into the lock on my cell door. With a twist, the door opened and swung inwards towards me.

He moved across the way, playing with the keys until he selected the right ones to unlock the cells for my friends, speaking the entire time he was moving.

"I wanted to load the bags for you, but I didn't think I'd make it undetected so this is the best I can do. I brought several changes of clothes, food, water, medical supplies, and put them in the backpacks. One for each of you," Fitz was saying as he freed my sister.

She stepped out of her cell warily and went to search the bags with Brayden to make sure Fitz was telling the truth, but I knew he was.

"The duffel bag has weapons in it. I grabbed a bunch, I don't know if everyone has the same skill set as Lexi here, but I put a lot of different things in there," Fitz continued as he got to Damion's door.

Damion stood very close to the door and Ally shook her head at him, encouraging him to (hopefully) not stab Fitz with the dart. He had already proved himself by releasing all of us and bringing us supplies.

Fitz put the key in and opened the door to Damion's cell, letting it swing open and giving Damion his freedom. Sensing that Damion was not fully sold on him yet, Fitz took a step back and even kept his hands up a little so that Damion could see he was unarmed.

The two of them stared at each other for a long minute before Damion reached his hand out in a handshake form towards Fitz.

"I'm Damion. Thank you for keeping my sister safe," Damion said as Fitz grasped his hand.

"Fitz," he answered with a nod, reintroducing himself. "So you're the other prince." Fitz turned to look at Ally and she stood up to face him. "That must make you..."

"Allyson," my sister answered. "But my friends call me Ally." She added that last part with a smile. "Our team-mates, Brayden and the big one is Yager."

Fitz nodded at both of them, and the two boys nodded back.

"This is a lot, man," Yager said as he analyzed the bags. "Thank you, sir." He reached out and shook Fitz's hand.

"We don't have a lot of time. The M.A. will be getting up soon and they'll definitely hear you when you leave," Fitz said.

"What is the plan?" I asked, realizing that he was arming us with weapons and supplies and I didn't know what was about to go down.

"Remember that old pickup truck next to the barn?" Fitz asked me.

I nodded.

"That's the best I can do for your ride out of here. The keys are in the truck. I don't know where they stashed your vehicles otherwise I would try to get those back to you," he continued, nodding at my teammates.

I remembered where Cole and I left our bikes on the outskirts of the kingdom. With any luck, they might still be there. We had some supplies in those as well which we might end up needing, but I wasn't sure how possible it would be to cross the town to get there.

"Our bikes are on the outskirts of the kingdom on the other side though," I said. "If we could get to them, we would have extra supplies."

"I'll try to get them and store them somewhere secretly until we meet again. But I recommend you take the truck and head north towards the mountains. Go through Mount Pleasant, but I promise you that there's nothing pleasant about it," Fitz explained. "I want you to get out safely, but I do hope we meet again. All of you."

He looked at me and each of my friends in turn with sincerity in his eyes and then he pulled a gun from his waistband.

We all froze for a millisecond before he spun the weapon around towards me in a gesture for me to take it.

"Are you giving this to me?" I asked.

"In order for them to not know that I let you all out, you're going to have to shoot me so it looks like you overpowered me and escaped," Fitz said.

"Shoot you?!" Ally said with a look of horror.

"It's one of the dart guns, and as Lexi knows, two shots to the chest will do it for me," Fitz answered, giving me another smile.

I returned his smile and then his words about where we were going registered in my head.

Mount Pleasant.

That could very well be where Remy is and that was where Cole and I wanted to go anyway.

Cole.

"Fitz, where is Cole?" I asked him.

"Um, I'm not sure. I haven't seen him since the party, but there's no way he suspects me helping you," Fitz answered.

"Ah. No," Damion said and held up a finger. "He's with us."

In the dim dungeon light, Fitz's face turned white.

"Wait, what do you mean?" he asked.

"He's ORC," I answered, deciding it was okay to let the truth out. "He's the other fugitive with me. We've been on the run together."

Fitz smacked his forehead.

"Of course. I should've known. You have all the same combat moves as him and I should've noticed that. Well, shame on us for letting him infiltrate our army too," Fitz said with a shrug.

"We'll find him before we leave," Yager said.

"Don't worry, Lex. We'll make sure he comes with us," Ally said and she came over to me to put an arm around me.

"You guys better hustle then, if you need to find him and get to the truck," Fitz said.

"We can't thank you enough," Damion said and shook Fitz's hand again. He walked over to me, giving me a quick hug and taking my hand before he grabbed a backpack and put one on as the rest of our team followed suit. Yager took two backpacks and Brayden carried the duffel bag with the weapons in it.

"Don't mention it," Fitz replied. "And I mean that. I don't want to blow my cover." He smiled again, like he was excited to be this double agent.

The team assembled behind me, leaving Fitz and I standing together.

"I'm so glad you walked into the barn that day and tried to shoot me," Fitz said to me. "You're a great friend and I hope you find someone equally as great as you."

"I already have. I just need to make sure he leaves with us," I answered with a small smile.

"Oh damn. You and Cole? You two are..." Fitz fumbled for his words and turned red. "I didn't know!"

"That's the point," I answered quietly.

"You have more secrets than anyone I've ever known," Fitz said.

"Stay strong. You're going to be a great Rank Leader, and we'll try to keep in touch if we can. Thank you for everything," I replied.

Fitz nodded and opened his arms for a hug. I hugged my new friend, knowing I would truly miss him.

"I said I owed you one and this is it," Fitz answered.

"You said you owed me two. So now there's only one favor left to be claimed," I replied and while hugging him, I took my dart and Damion's dart that he had passed back to me and held them together in my right hand. I gave Fitz an extra tight squeeze and plunged them both into his back. I felt the tears prick at my eyes but they didn't spill over as I quite literally stabbed my friend in the back.

I held onto Fitz as his legs sagged and I lowered him to the ground as gently as I could so that he was laying on his side. The two darts were still protruding from his shirt as the tranquilizing serum spread through his body.

"Nice one," he said quietly and I could tell he was fighting sleep. "I didn't even see that one coming."

Fitz smiled at me and closed his eyes. His head lolled to the side and he was out.

"See you soon, my friend," I said to his sleeping form.

I took in a breath and turned back to my team.

"Let's go," I said to them.

"Lead the way," Damion said and gestured past him towards the exit.

I swept past him towards the door but not before throwing one last look at Fitz who was sleeping peacefully on the floor of the dungeon. If only our escape could go that smoothly and peacefully too...

21

I led my former teammates, now back to my current teammates, through the depths of the castle until we reached familiar territory on the main floor.

I was surprised to find that the door that led to the dungeon where we were being held was just an average looking door near the hallway that led to the staff quarters. We had retreated from the dank dungeon, up several sets of stairs and down multiple hallways until I opened the last door to the carpeted floors that I was used to. How strange that it was kept so central to the highly trafficked halls of the castle.

This also made this next part challenging, since there was a high probability of us running into someone that we didn't want to.

I wasn't sure where the current staff members, like Rita, Thomas, or Brooke stood, so I was unsure whether they were to be labeled as a friend or foe. But I was holding Fitz' dart gun low and leading our team, deciding that if it had to be fired, I would be the one to do it.

Brayden gave me a crash course in guns, and this small handheld one that I was holding. I was thankful to have him on this team and even though we had moved past our differences, I imagined that taking a step back and allowing me to lead was not easy for him.

We turned one last corner and I saw the double doors ahead that led us to the staff quarters. I had stood here only hours ago before Oliver took me down. The halls had been quiet and as we passed windows, it looked to have been shortly before dawn as the sky was beginning to turn pink and orange far away on the horizon.

I opened one of the doors slowly and slid through it, allowing my team time to follow. I held up a fist to indicate that we should stop forward motion and my friends all followed my order. I took a few steps away from them towards my room and opened the door, aiming my weapon as I did so, but no one was in there to jump out at me.

The room had been ransacked. The little clothes that I had were tossed about, drawers were hanging open and the mattress was not quite on the bed anymore. I looked around and let out a sigh, knowing that my bag or any of my few possessions were not here.

I quietly backed out of the room and rejoined my team. My weapon was out in front of me as we slowly walked, careful not to make too much noise and to alert anyone to our presence. We passed our living area and our kitchen, both of which were deserted. I hurried along, knowing that sometimes the staff got up early and we did not want to be found here with very few options of escape.

We came up to the back door that would lead us out towards the barn and the truck that we were looking for. I turned around to reassess my team of four and they were all still with me.

I twisted the knob and peered through the crack out the door. The outdoor gardens were quiet. I listened intently and heard... still nothing.

I assumed that the M.A. expected us to be in the dungeon still, so they likely weren't on high alert, or expecting us to have escaped and wandering the grounds.

I held onto the doorknob and turned to my team.

"Okay," I whispered. "We're going to run. Quickly and quietly, and follow me. I'll lead us to the barn where the truck is, then we will take a small team to go to the Lodge and search for Cole while the others ready the truck. Got it?"

I was met with four nodding heads.

No questions worked for me so I pushed open the door and started to run. I ran straight ahead, taking the most direct pathway and sweeping my eyes left and right looking for anyone who might be on patrol.

The only sounds still were our footsteps, our breathing, and the occasional sounds of crickets or creatures coming from the trees around us. I ran through the dangerously open field until I got to the barn and slid my body around the corner of the structure. I peeked in through the side door and upon seeing the place empty, pulled it open and ran inside.

My ribs screamed in pain from that much movement but it was the price to pay to get out of here.

Damion and Ally filed in shortly after me, followed by Yager and then Brayden with his bow out and arrow drawn. He surveyed each corner of the barn, aiming his weapon at every alcove and once satisfied, he lowered it towards the ground and let out a huff of air.

"Lexi, who do you want to take to find Monahan?" Brayden asked as he dropped his bags he was carrying. My team and I followed suit as it would be much easier to move without all of that extra weight.

"I'll go," Ally offered. "I can help track him."

"Then I'm going with you," Damion said protectively.

"Cole won't know that you're all here and on his side," I said and then paused. "Probably best if it's not you right now, Damion... he did get you in the face before."

"Don't remind me," my brother answered with an eye roll. "I had a headache for a week after his escape. But you're right."

"I'll go," Yager said. "Brayden and Damion can load up the truck, take stock of what we have in the bags and keep an eye out for anyone. We should be back soon."

"Okay, that works," I answered. "Ally, you take this." I handed her the dart gun although I knew she had a knife strapped to her leg and her ankle but I wanted her to have a little bit of extra protection.

I had my new bow, courtesy of Fitz, and Yager had... well... himself, which was threatening enough.

"Be careful," Damion said as he and Brayden set to work moving the bags towards the truck.

"You too," I replied and I took my tiny team of three and headed towards the Lodge.

We crept out of the barn and I was thankful to be under tree coverage relatively quickly. I stayed on the outskirts as long as I could before I had to cut in towards the Lodge itself. It was going to get more dangerous the closer we got to the Lodge so I was moving a little slower and using extra caution. I wasn't sure how they bumped up their security since the "break in," but I wasn't going to take any chances.

And good thing too.

I held up my fist just in time as my carefully trained eyes caught a glint of something running between two trees at about knee level. I bent down to examine it and it was a thin string of some sort. I didn't touch it but upon closer inspection it was shiny and looked like it might be a wire.

I was hesitant to find out what would happen if we had walked through it and triggered it so I took a careful and deliberate step over it and indicated to Ally and Yager to do the same.

They both stepped over the obstacle with no problem and we left it behind us, but I made a mental note to remember it on the way back.

I wasn't sure how we would even find Cole. I made the assumption that he had to be here at the Lodge but then again, what if he wasn't? He should be somewhere far away from Nate but perhaps the Lodge wasn't the best place.

I couldn't leave with my team and leave without Cole. It would destroy me. It had already been hard enough when we were only apart for a few weeks or less, so I decided it was not an option for me to leave here without him. I would stay and fight my way through every M.A. member if I had to, no matter what the odds were.

"Lexi!" I heard Ally hiss from behind me.

I stopped and spun around to face her. I hadn't been paying attention and I wasn't even sure if that was the first time she had called my name. Judging by her expression, it was not.

I didn't see her immediately and realized her voice came from above me where her and Yager were sitting in neighboring trees. She waved at me hurriedly and I took two steps to prepare to launch myself upward when I heard the twigs snap in a close proximity to me.

I froze and then ducked to the side, putting the trunk of a particularly rounded tree between myself and the snapping twig. I looked down at my feet to make sure that I wasn't about to step on any particularly crunchy foliage and I readied my weapon. I had my bow aimed slightly downward because I decided even though these people were the enemy, a shot to the leg was much more likely to heal than a shot to the torso, and I didn't want to become a killer.

I listened as the intruder (I was able to distinguish that it was just one person) moved slowly through the trees and seemed to be heading towards us and coming from the Lodge.

I held my breath as I heard them pass me and head underneath where Ally and Yager were hiding. I didn't hear the *pew!* of Ally's weapon firing or any sounds from

Yager so I was unsure why she didn't take out our opponent.

When I finally was able to look around the opposite side of the tree to get a glimpse of our opponent, I understood why and I made a choice at that moment.

"Ellis," I said, revealing myself from behind the tree. I emerged with my arrow drawn and aimed right at her.

She whipped around quickly to face me, her hair in its signature bun and it only wobbled slightly when she turned to face me.

"Lexi!" she said with a smile when she finally saw me. Then her smile faded at the sight of the weapon in my hand.

I was pretty sure she was on my side, but I wasn't going to jeopardize the safety of my teammates because I was pretty sure and not one hundred percent certain.

"Please don't shoot me," she squeaked and put her hands up.

I was silent for a minute, sizing her up and she looked... terrified. If she was some sort of double agent, like I had originally thought when I met Ally, then she was either the worst or the best because she looked so frightened.

She kept opening and closing her eyes and flinching away from me like I was going to let the arrow go at any second. Her hands remained in the air next to her ears and were trembling.

I lowered my arrow, knowing that Ally was likely taking aim in case she needed to. As I lowered my weapon, I made a quick fist with my hand hoping that Ally and Yager would see that, and not reveal themselves or shoot her as I lowered my arrow.

"I'm so glad that you're okay," Ellis whispered to me, her hands shaking slightly less. "I couldn't believe what Nate and Oliver did to you and I'm sorry I couldn't help you."

I took a step towards her and looked at her. Her bun was flawless as usual but something looked different about it that I couldn't pinpoint. Upon closer examination of my friend, I noticed that she had a slight purple discoloration on the side of her face that I hadn't noticed when I was hiding behind the tree.

"Ellis, who hit you?" I asked her, now with my bow pointed completely at the ground.

"No one. It's... it's fine," she said quietly.

"Ellis. You have to tell me who hit you," I repeated.

I heard her choke back a sob and she whispered her answer. "Nate."

The sob emerged and I looked around to make sure that we were still alone, and we were.

"He... he hit me. After he darted you, I tried uselessly to get to you and help. He hit me so hard that I fell backwards. They left me there on the floor. Oliver didn't do anything to help me, he just picked you up and carried you away. I'm sorry I couldn't help you," Ellis explained through a few more quiet sobs. I appreciated the effort I could see her exuding to keep her sobs at an appropriate level for escaped prisoners.

"You did what you could and that was very brave," I said to her. "Thank you for trying."

"I've been looking for you," Ellis said suddenly, putting me on guard again. "Cole is hiding in my room. I got him safely there after they tore apart your room, figuring they wouldn't look for him there. It came out that Nate knew he was here and he wasn't who he said he was so everyone is looking for him currently."

"Why didn't you turn him in?" I asked.

"I didn't believe them about you, and if you love him, then I believe you about who he is," Ellis answered. She put her hands on her hips and looked at me like she was proud of herself.

I finally realized why her hair looked different. The ribbon that was wrapping it up was a dark purple instead of blue. It reminded me of the color of my bike.

Ellis did not miss the movement as my eyes flicked up to her bun and then back to her face. And she smiled at me.

"I borrowed this from you," she said pointing to the ribbon. "I was hoping it would show you that I'm on your side. And I may have gotten this out before your room was ransacked." She turned away from me and showed me the item on her back.

My backpack from Cole.

The purple ribbon in her hair was from my bag and I saw her blue ribbon tied in its place onto my bag.

"My backpack," I breathed and I closed the space between Ellis and I.

I grabbed her and I hugged her over my backpack while still holding my weapon, but I was careful. She returned my hug with just as much squeeze as I gave her.

"Prince Joseph told me he was bringing you supplies and getting you out so I filled your bag with whatever I thought you would need," Ellis said and moved to take the bag off.

"Please hold onto that for me," I said, holding out my hand. "We'll get you back to safety and then figure out how to get you back into the castle undetected."

"We?" Ellis asked, looking around.

On cue, Ally and Yager dropped from the tree behind me and flanked both sides of me. Ellis took a step back as I'm sure they looked a little intimidating, dropping in unexpectedly like that.

I turned to my team.

"We get Cole, we get Ellis back to safety and we get out. Got it?" I asked.

I got two nods in return again.

"Ellis, behind me," I said to her. "They'll bring up the rear, making sure we are covered." I hesitated introducing her to Ally and Yager, in case they questioned her after our escape. I wanted her to have as little information as possible.

Ellis clung close to me as we trekked back through the woods and away from the Lodge. I stopped us at the appropriate times and navigated us over and around those mysterious trip wires and we made it to the treeline unscathed.

The sky was really starting to glow orange now and the sun would be peeking over the horizon very soon. We were losing the cover of darkness to mask our escape so we would have to pick up the pace.

My injured ribs protested against my movements as I picked up my pace into a jog, but I ignored the pain and continued on. Ellis kept pace with me and I could hear Ally and Yager close behind us.

We approached the edge of the trees and I nocked an arrow (just in case) as we broke through the treeline and started to jog across the open field to the barn.

The sun had made its appearance now and the tendrils of light were spreading across the field, engulfing the grass and all structures around it in its warm glow. I felt its warmth on my face and inhaled a deep breath through my nose as we jogged.

I turned around to make sure Ally and Yager were close when I caught a flash of red emerging from the trees behind us, followed by a humming whizzing sound.

"Get down!" I shouted and threw Ellis to the ground as an arrow flew past where she was just standing and landed in the grass about twenty feet from us. I looked at where the arrow landed, thankful that it didn't hit any of us when it suddenly exploded.

It shook the ground and brought Ally and Yager to the ground. Dirt and grass showered us and I covered Ellis with my body.

"The hell was that?!" Yager shouted.

I got to my feet first and fired a few shots at the treeline and made eye contact with Nate who was on one knee and taking aim at us.

He dodged my arrows easily at such a far distance and mine didn't explode like his did.

"Targets on the lawn, they have a hostage. Backup requested now!" Nate yelled into his radio with a smile.

"Time to go!" Ally said and she pulled Ellis to her feet and started running with her, leaving Yager and I behind. I would have been offended, but Ally knew that my priority was Ellis' safety.

Yager and I jumped up and started running towards the barn and we both could only hope that Damion and Brayden were basically ready to go.

Arrows whizzed past us heading back towards Nate and I looked up to see Brayden standing at the corner of the barn and taking a few shots to provide us with cover. He waved us onward frantically and I pumped my legs as fast as they would allow me with my injury.

Yager slid around the corner and Brayden grabbed me and pulled me behind some barrels providing us cover.

"You good, Probie?" he asked, examining me for any injuries.

"I'm fine, Cole is in the staff quarters. We need to get to him," I said.

"I'll tell the others," Brayden said. "Cover us." He nodded towards the treeline where Nate was advancing on us much too quickly, although I didn't see any M.A. members bursting into the field yet.

I turned to Brayden.

"You keep Ellis safe!" I shouted at him before he ducked around to the other side of the structure.

I turned around just as the barrel that I was hiding behind exploded, sending me flying backwards and also sending hundreds of wooden pieces into the air.

I landed on my back. Hard.

All of the air rushed from my lungs and I felt pain everywhere when I landed. I rolled over onto my side, coughing and trying to pull in breaths of air. I looked up to see Nate running right towards me, his bow over his shoulder and a knife in his hand.

He launched through the air and I rolled over onto my side as he brought the knife down in the space my body had just been. I rolled over again and dodged his next blow.

"You're full of surprises," he said to me. "How did you escape?"

"Hit the guard with a dart you failed to take out of my pocket after you guys threw me down there," I explained, trying to make it seem like Fitz didn't help us. Although I was fairly certain no one expected that he did help us.

Nate launched himself at me again and clipped my arm with his blade. I let out a hiss and grabbed at my wound, feeling the blood seep through my fingers.

"You've lost your touch. Hiding out here... as a maid?" he taunted me and came for me again but I was ready.

I pushed his arm away and planted a kick in his midsection, causing him to double over. I dropped my elbow down between his shoulder blades, and swept his feet out from under him and he hit the ground.

I took a few steps backwards to give me some distance and I looked up to see several M.A. members come out from the trees. They would reach us in minutes.

Nate still hadn't gotten to his feet, but I didn't want to take any chances. I approached him and wrapped my arm around his neck and pressed with my other hand on his other carotid artery, knowing he would pass out in a few moments.

He tried to stand up and throw himself backwards unexpectedly. He only got to one foot but he threw himself onto the ground and I was behind him so I took the brunt of the fall with his body on top of mine. I heard him suck in mouthfuls of air before he spun on me and punched me right in the face.

My head whipped back into the grass and I saw stars. My vision wasn't even clear yet before Nate hit me again and I felt the blackness creeping in the edges of my vision. One or two more of those and I would definitely be out.

I brought my hands up to protect myself but Nate was faster and stronger, and he had leverage with his body on top of mine. He grabbed both of my hands in one of his and pushed them to the side and gave me a quick slap across the face.

I let out a gasp as it always surprised me when someone did that. The last time, having been Queen Camilla, herself.

"That's for all of the trouble you caused me," Nate said.

I shook my head and he pressed my hands into the grass above me and leaned down close to me.

"I don't care if your mother said to bring you in alive," Nate said. "I could say it was self defense and you attacked me."

"You. Are. A. Monster," I said to him between clenched teeth. I was straining against him but he was bigger, stronger, and I was weakened.

"You'll beg for me to kill you," he whispered to me and then leaned down and pressed his lips to mine.

I bucked my hips and tried to move out from under his grasp but I was stuck. I was mortified, horrified, disgusted, and I needed this animal off of me. I whipped my head forward and smacked my forehead into his head. It hurt me, but I hoped that it hurt him more.

Nate growled and then quicker than a flash of light, he punched me right in the ribcage.

I screamed in pain at my already injured body being hit again. Surely something had to be broken now. I felt the tears fill my eyes at the pain and I closed them, willing them not to fall and show my weakness. It was too late though as the first tears slid out of the sides of my eyes.

Suddenly Nate's weight was off of me and I opened my eyes to see the space above me empty and he was gone. I sat up, my midsection screaming at me and I pressed a hand to my ribs which caused me excruciating pain as well. There had to be some serious internal damage.

I looked over to see Nate and another figure tossing and turning. I rolled myself onto my side, my arm giving out from holding me up and felt myself shed more tears as I examined the scene before me.

Cole.

He was engaged in a fierce round of hand to hand combat with Nate and was matching him perfectly. Nate still had his knife and was brandishing it at Cole.

I felt my quiver beneath me, probably left a bruise under that too from landing on it and I reached around to feel that I had a few arrows left. I searched the ground around me for my bow and saw it a few feet away.

With zero ability to move my abdominal muscles without it causing excruciating pain, I was rolling and using my arms to pull me across the grass to my bow.

I heard Nate and Cole exchange threatening words and the occasional grunt when one of them landed a blow but they were evenly matched and it would be challenging to land a hit on the other.

Finally I crawled to my bow and picked up, scooping up one of the arrows from the ground near it. This arrow was black and smooth like mine, but the feathered end, had a thick red line wrapping around the arrow.

My eyes widened.

Was this one of Nate's exploding arrows?

I drew it back in my bow and launched it towards the approaching M.A. members rather than Nate, who was dangerously close to the man that I loved. The arrow did indeed explode a few feet from the incoming army so I launched a few more at them, creating a line of fiery explosions and putting a barrier between us and them... for now.

I turned back to the fight behind me, just as Nate was about to plunge his knife into Cole, who was laying face down on his stomach.

"No!" I screamed and grabbed an arrow from my quiver and shot it directly for Nate's torso. It struck him right between the shoulder blades in his back.

There was a silent moment that none of us moved. Then Nate dropped his knife and tipped over to the side.

"Cole!" I called. "Cole! Are you okay!"

There was another agonizingly slow minute before Cole finally moved and pushed himself onto his hands and knees. He shook his head and looked around to see Nate lying on his side, his eyes closed. Then he looked around until he saw me and the bow in my hand.

Cole was at my side in a minute.

"Lexi, are you okay? Geez, your face," he said to me and started dabbing my nose and my lip with his sleeve.

"You mean I don't look beautiful?" I asked with a smile and I felt my lip split open... again.

"Always," Cole said and cupped my face with his hands and kissed me. It stung when he pressed his hands to my face and his lips to mine but this pain was worth it to be with him and be this close to him.

"Hey, lovebirds!" Brayden called to us. I opened my eyes to see him running over towards us. "More of that later, we gotta go!"

I started to scoop up as many of Nate's red arrows as I could find and put them into my quiver. Cole followed suit until Brayden got close enough to us and helped me off of the ground. I put an arm around each of them, although surely Cole could've carried me by himself and wobbled around the barn to where the truck was waiting.

I thought my side of the barn where I just had my fight with Nate was bad, but the front of the barn looked worse. There were arrows sticking out of the barn front and M.A. members funneling out of the castle towards us at an alarming speed.

"Oh yes, time to go," I said. "Where's Ellis? Is she safe?"

"She's still in the barn," Brayden answered. "I couldn't get her to the castle. She would've been hit."

"She can't stay there, Lexi," Cole said. "They'll know she helped us."

"Then what do we do?" I asked.

"Take me with you," Ellis said from the side doorway to the barn.

"Ellis, I would never ask you to leave your home," I said to my friend, still leaning on Brayden and Cole.

"I know, and you didn't ask. I volunteered. I want to come. There's nothing left for me here now," Ellis answered.

I looked at Cole and Brayden and both of them shrugged.

"She'd be safer with us and you know it," Brayden said.

"Agreed," Cole said with a nod.

"Then it's settled. I'm coming," Ellis answered and put her hands on her hips for the second time today. "Plus, I have your backpack, Lexi." She patted it on her back safely.

"Great. Let's get to the truck. Are we good to go?" I asked.

"Should be. Damion got it up and running and it's loaded up although a few of us are going to have to lie down in the bed of the truck," Brayden said.

Another explosion shook the barn and Ellis came running out of the barn to join us.

"I'll give cover with Nate's exploding arrows so we can get to the truck. It's mostly hidden from view so shouldn't be too risky," I offered.

"I'll do it," Brayden said. "You're injured and I just might be a better shot than you."

I let out a snort and then covered my mouth in embarrassment. I started to laugh and then doubled over at the pain that laughing caused me with my injury.

"Correction: Very injured. Get her and Ellis in first, followed by Ally and the rest of us," Brayden ordered and let go of me. He slid my quiver off with such precision and looped it around his own shoulder so that he was sporting two of them. "Get them in, Cole."

Cole picked me up in one smooth motion. I cried out at the surprise and the pain in my ribs as he made a run for the truck. We heard a few whizzing sounds as arrows flew but Cole was quick and their aim was poor.

He unceremoniously tossed me into the backseat of the truck and I cried out again. He threw me an apologetic look and dashed across the opening again to help cover Ellis. She only had to make it about twenty feet but she was not nearly as quick as any of us who had training.

Yager and Ally suddenly sprinted from the front of the barn and he covered my sister as she dove into the backseat beside me. She looked me over.

"You look terrible," she said to me. I stuck my tongue out at her, and upon her realizing I was okay, climbed into the front passenger seat to give Ellis some room for when she likely came running in at full speed.

I looked towards the back of the barn where the smoke was thick from where I built us a wall from the exploding arrows to keep the army members out. I looked the other direction where there were now swarms of army members closing in and getting closer by using trees and other landmarks as shields.

Cole gave Ellis a push to run as Brayden laid down cover fire to the front, keeping arrows from flying at my friend. With her bun bouncing, Ellis started her run towards me.

"ELLIS!" a male voice hollered.

Ellis stopped running just over the halfway point and she looked to her left which was towards the back of the barn. There hadn't been any people there so we weren't providing cover and there stood Oliver with his gun pointed at her.

"You are a traitor!" Oliver shouted at her.

Her pause in her run was all he needed to fire off several shots at her.

"No!" I screamed as everything happened in slow motion.

Yager was somehow on her in the second before Oliver's shots struck her. He grabbed her small frame and threw her to the ground and she landed ungracefully on her back. He kept his body above hers, shielding her from Oliver's advance.

Their faces were so close, they practically could be touching noses. I watched as Yager's body twitched a little with each dart (phew, nothing deadly) that buried itself in his torso and Ellis reached up and put her hands on his face and said something to him that I couldn't hear over the chaos.

Brayden spun immediately and planted an arrow (a regular one, thankfully) right into Oliver's shoulder and he dropped his weapon, and stumbled backwards until he fell onto his back. I watched as his limbs were still moving and he grabbed for his shoulder to stop the blood flow.

I looked back to see Yager carrying Ellis in his arms towards the truck until he collapsed a foot short of the vehicle.

"Ellis, get inside!" I shouted but my friend didn't budge as she tried to pick up Yager.

"You need to stand!" she was shouting at him and pulling on his arms, but Yager was too large for her to move him by herself.

Brayden was providing us excellent coverage therefore despite the protests my body made when I moved, I pushed off the cushioned backseat and threw myself out of the truck and onto the ground. I landed on my hands and knees, gasped in pain, and started to pluck the darts out of Yager and flick them away. I pulled three from his torso and one from his left thigh and I could see him fighting to move his right leg to stand on it. It was a miracle he was even still conscious at all.

Ally was by my side in a minute and it took everything that Ally, Ellis, and I had to pull Yager up to standing and push him into the backseat that I had just vacated.

"A little more, Yager, come on!" Ally said as she pushed his left leg up into the vehicle.

The three of us ungracefully handled the large man and awkwardly shoved him in the backseat.

"Get in with him," I said to Ellis and she followed my orders, immediately hopping up next to Yager and pulling the door shut. I didn't even have to tell her to stay down, but she lowered her body, keeping her head below the windows in case any stray shots came this way.

A figure crawling out from under the truck caused me to shriek and jump away but I realized it was only Damion.

"Are we ready to roll? I'm not enjoying this anymore," he said to me as he pulled himself out from under the truck and opened the door. "Ally, slide over."

My sister jumped in and slid over to the passenger seat and Damion took the driver's seat.

Yager's body was taking over the entire backseat so I would have to jump in the back of the truck with Cole and Brayden, which was fine by me. A little bit of grunting later, I had scaled the side of the truck and rolled my body into the bed.

"Guys!" Damion called to our remaining team members. "Let's go!"

"Cover us!" Brayden shouted as he and Cole ducked their heads and ran across the gap towards us.

I picked up a bow from the back of the truck and began firing off shots to keep the M.A. from closing in on us any further.

Brayden continued to fire a few shots here and there, but I was doing the majority of the cover work to get them to us safely. He closed the remaining distance and vaulted himself over the side of the pick-up and into the back with me, rocking the truck slightly.

Cole leapt to copy Brayden's movements but his body twisted awkwardly in the air and he fell short of the truck, landing on his stomach.

"Cole!" I cried and leaned over the edge of the truck. He was laying on the ground but pushing himself to his hands and knees, despite the arrow that was protruding out of his lower back. I gasped at the sight of it and wondered how I missed covering him. I whipped my head in the other direction, the side I hadn't been covering as much, where Oliver had been.

I saw Oliver laying on his side, working his hands around the arrow that Brayden had shot him with but he was not paying us any attention. And then coming up behind him towards us, with an evil scowl, was Nate.

"I was aiming for you, Lexi!" Nate shouted at me as he pulled another arrow into his bow.

"I'd take an arrow for you, any day," Cole said to me as he slowly got to his feet and turned towards Nate.

"Guess that'll just take you both out... finally," Nate said and he pointed his arrow at the ground and stopped next to Oliver.

I realized what his words meant when I looked at the arrow that was still in Cole's back.

"Cole! It's a red arrow! It's going to explode!" I shouted at him, frantically. I knew we shouldn't pull it out but with the other option being... not as great, it was the best choice. We only had seconds before it exploded and would likely kill Cole in the process.

Cole reached his hand up behind him and tugged on the arrow and growled in pain as he did so, bringing him to one of his knees. The angle wasn't right and he was having a hard time pulling the arrow out. He spun away from us as he gripped the arrow one more time and snapped the end with the red right off. Cole pulled his arm back and threw the arrow as far as he could with all of the strength he had left.

But the arrow didn't get far enough.

It exploded mere feet from Cole and the force of the explosion launched him backwards into the truck. His body hit the truck with such force, it seemed to rock sideways and suspend on two wheels for a moment before it returned to the ground.

I didn't see where or how his body hit the truck as Brayden grabbed me and pulled me down, throwing his body on top of mine in the process. He was still covering me as the smoke from the explosion was beginning to clear. I gave him a shove and he climbed off of me and the two of us leaned over the side of the truck.

"Dammit!" Brayden hissed and immediately leapt out of the truck.

Arrows flew and darts flew and by some stroke of luck, Brayden did not get hit. Then suddenly the arrows stopped flying.

I looked to my side and saw Ally sitting on the open passenger side window as she fired the dart gun and dropped Nate and his bow to his knees right next to Oliver.

My hands were shaking as I watched Brayden throw Cole's lifeless body over his shoulder and using the tire for leverage, climb into the bed of the truck with me. He laid him down on the floor next to me and I raked my eyes over the sight of him.

Cole's eyes were closed, the clothes on the front of him were shredded and I could see pieces of the arrow sticking out of his flesh through his torn clothing. There was blood everywhere and the skin on his torso was already blistering from the fiery explosion. Brayden had to lean him towards one side since the remaining half of the arrow was still protruding from his back, and blood was pouring out of the wound around it.

I pressed my fingers to the side of his neck and prayed and hoped that I would feel something. Anything to know that he wasn't gone.

I switched to the other side of his neck, tears falling freely down my face, the salt stinging the many cuts that covered my face and my lips from Nate's assault, but I didn't care. All that mattered was that I felt something. Anything.

After much too long, I finally felt it. It was weak and thready but a pulse fluttered faintly under my fingers and I began to sob.

"Cole," I mumbled through my tears. "Please wake up."

"Is he…" Brayden whispered to me.

"He has a pulse, but look at the shape he's in. It'll take a miracle to fix him," I said, still openly crying.

"Thank goodness we have you to fix him then," Brayden said and placed a hand on my shoulder reassuringly. "I know you of all people can work a miracle."

I continued to keep both of my hands wrapped around one of Cole's as I heard Brayden smack the window above us to the back of the truck to indicate to Damion that he should drive and my brother wasted no time as he pressed on the accelerator.

I didn't lift my head up for fear of being hit with one of the flying projectiles still but once the M.A. was out of range, I did lift my head and steal one last look at the castle. It loomed large and somehow unthreatening in the distance as the sun, which had now emerged completely, covered it in a golden hue.

I turned my head around to see Ellis poking her head up over the top of the seat and also staring at the castle. I hoped she was happy with her choice to come with us, although as soon as Oliver publicly named her a traitor, I would've tossed her into the truck myself. I remembered the way she and Yager looked at each other, and I would be lying if I said I didn't hope that scary moment for them ignited a spark or two.

Yager was finally unconscious and I expected him to be out for a while after being hit with those darts. His large size probably helped him fight off the sedative longer than the average person. He had the biggest heart and I knew that he would be okay after he woke up. And it certainly didn't hurt that he had Ellis keeping an extra close eye on him.

Damion held our course steady as we flew over grassy fields, hopefully heading for some sort of road or path to make the ride less bumpy. He emerged as a natural leader throughout all of this, and I was glad that he was on our team, leading with Brayden. I remembered they were co-leading our team when we first left Odessa, which felt like ages ago.

Brayden also really stepped up as a leader, a soldier, and a friend throughout all of this. I remembered our rocky start when I accidentally shot him with the paint pellets on that first night and how he had definitely marked me down as trouble after that. Now we were getting better; he seemed to be more comfortable around me, and perhaps he was forgetting my royal roots which made him overly cordial toward me. It had sort of made me miss the banter that we had before, but I saw it starting to reemerge after everything that we had been through.

Ally sat in the passenger seat eyes trained ahead, her stare hard and serious. She seemed to be concentrating intently and looked to the side mirrors occasionally to make sure that we were not being followed, which so far, we were clear. Her combat skills and even her work with the dart gun was impressive and she had improved so much in the short time that we were apart when I was in Middletown and they were looking for me. It would be a long road for her and Damion, coming to terms with the truth about their, or rather, *our* mother but I hoped that it would just take time.

Finally, I looked down at the man I loved again and pressed my hand to his cheek. Cole and I had been through so much together and even though it felt like the bad was currently outweighing the good, as long as he was here, alive, and with me, he would be one of the good things that would never tip the scale against me.

I lifted my hand off of his cheek and brushed my own hair out of my face, knowing that I had to get started working on him now before his condition got any worse. I could only hope that he would forgive me for the amount of pain I was likely to cause him from removing that arrow from his back and suturing his many wounds, including a large gash on the back of his head from when he slammed into the truck.

I thought about my friends and siblings riding along in this old pick-up truck with me. They would have never been in this situation if it wasn't for me, but I tried not to dwell on that. They were here now and I was determined to keep every single person that I cared about alive.

I looked at the road ahead as we drove on during the daylight wondering where we would end up. Fitz had told us to head towards Mount Pleasant, but had also warned us not to be fooled by its name. I didn't know if that meant it would have harsh conditions, harsh people, or both. I wasn't exactly eager to find out.

But I was glad to have teammates here to support me, and Ellis as our new addition. With a little bit of work, she just might become ORC material, but of course, we would give her that choice, if she wanted to learn.

I looked to the sky and felt the warm sun on my dirty, blood-covered face. I closed my eyes, took in a breath of the fresh, cool air and let it out slowly.

I opened my eyes and looked toward my next challenge. Healing Cole.

I rolled up my sleeves and the gears in my mind began to turn as I thought about the things I would need, along with the steps I would take. I just hoped that they were the right ones, because Cole's life depended on it. He was depending on me.

As we continued to speed away from the kingdom of Middletown, I had only one thought.

I would not fail.

THE ADVENTURE CONTINUES...

Lexi Palmer's journey is far from over.

See where her adventures take her next in the newest installment of The ORC Series:

The Medic

Coming May 2022!

AUTHOR'S NOTE

Thanks for reading!

A huge thank you to my editor, Bekah for being my extra eyes, my sounding board, and reminding me to take breaks when they were needed.

If you enjoyed reading this book, please spread the word and help other readers find it. You could start by leaving a review on Amazon or Goodreads or any other social media site. The review doesn't have to be long at all, but I take the time to read all of my reviews and appreciate each one of them!

ABOUT THE AUTHOR

Julie Falango

Julie Falango is a Registered Nurse by day, fiction writer by night. While she's been writing since grade school, she picked up writing more seriously as a way to escape the challenges and heartbreak of being a nurse during the COVID-19 pandemic. Creating stories she enjoyed helped her cope and she quickly realized that the escape might help others as well. Her young adult stories offer daring adventures, hope, and twists and turns that'll keep readers guess- ing until the final page.

Julie currently resides in Delaware and continues to work as a nurse and an author, although she uses a computer now instead of the spiral notebooks she wrote in as a child. When she's not working, she can be found reading and writing stories as well as music, watching sports, and going to the beach with friends. She hopes to entertain readers while running them through every emotion in her multi-faceted, complex stories.

Fans can connect with her on Instagram by following her at @jnf.author

Made in the USA
Columbia, SC
12 April 2022

58879751R00153